Matthew's mouth went bone dry

And it had nothing to do with thirst. And everything to do with Rachel, who had come to a halt beside him. "I take it this is the *intimate apparel* section in the shop," he bit out, his voice husky.

"Yes, this area is one of our most popular sections," Rachel murmured.

Following her, Matthew glanced at the selection of lingerie, his gaze connecting with a skimpy creation called a merry widow. Matthew couldn't stop himself from imagining how luscious Rachel would look in the garment's strapless top with black garters tipped with satin roses. In a heartbeat, his body started to respond.

Damn, he'd always controlled his libido as effectively as he controlled everything else in his life. Until now. Suddenly he knew that he had to leave. *Now.* Before he did something truly inexcusable. Like grabbing Rachel and kissing the hell out of her...and kissing their business partnership goodbye.

Somehow business—his passion—didn't seem nearly as appealing as crushing Rachel in his arms and teaching her a thing or two about mergers....

Dear Reader,

Welcome to another New Year filled with love and laughter! This month Stephanie Bond begins a hilarious duet featuring a hero and heroine who end up with exactly what they don't want. In *KIDS Is a 4-Letter Word* the last thing the heroine wants is children, so, of course, you know what happens. Next month some of the characters from the first book continue in their own funny and romantic story, *WIFE Is a 4-Letter Word.*

A New Year is also a good time to welcome another new author into the LOVE & LAUGHTER lineup. Sharon Stewart has a warm, amusing voice and she tells the charming story of a man who hates romance and a woman who has dedicated her life to it! Merriment and confused emotions ensue.

We have lots more wonderful books, lots of love and laughter planned for all of 1998.

Wishing you all the best for a wonderful New Year,

Malle Vallik

Malle Vallik
Associate Senior Editor

LOVE FOR SALE
Sharon Stewart

Harlequin Books

TORONTO • NEW YORK • LONDON
AMSTERDAM • PARIS • SYDNEY • HAMBURG
STOCKHOLM • ATHENS • TOKYO • MILAN
MADRID • WARSAW • BUDAPEST • AUCKLAND

ISBN 0-373-44036-7

LOVE FOR SALE

A funny thing happened...

Born and raised in Chicago, Sharon Stewart once dreamed of dancing for a living. Instead, she surrendered to life's more practical aspects, became a secretary and concentrated on typing and being a rabid Chicago Bears fan. Strange as it seems, Sharon never considered writing romance fiction until she moved to Phoenix, Arizona, and met Pierce Brosnan at a local shopping mall. It was a chance meeting that changed her life, because it sparked her to ask, *What if?* What if two fictional characters had met in the same way? That scenario formed the basis for this, her first novel. Sharon is now cheerfully addicted to writing contemporary romance and playing *What if?*

For the wonderful women of the Bookend Book Group,
partners on a memorable journey to Jerome.

1

THE ORNATELY LETTERED sign over the store entrance read Love Can Build A Bridge To Happiness. Matthew Kent knew it was a bunch of hogwash. Love—or the sentimental drivel people referred to as love—was a fool's illusion, he thought as he pushed open the door with one large hand.

He had learned *that* the hard way.

A small bell chimed merrily as he stepped through the doorway and into the Realm of Romance shop. The air was filled with a delicate floral scent, and the whisper-soft sound of violins could be heard in the background. Matthew glanced around him, a grim expression settling on his face. It was even worse than he had imagined when he'd seen the vividly painted outside of the old, three-story brick house. Unbelievable! A business totally devoted to romance, right in the center of the historic city of Jerome, Arizona.

And he could own this house—a *pink* house, for God's sake!—and a half interest in the store that occupied the ground floor, *if* he complied with the terms of his Aunt Ava's will. Since his mother's older sister had been one of the "flighty McCarthys," as his father had derisively nicknamed that side of the family, Lord only knew what those terms would be. Well, he'd find out when the will was read tomorrow. Then he'd have to decide what to do.

"I'll be right with you," a female voice called cheerfully through an open doorway at the rear.

"That's okay. Take your time," he called back, and

hoped she would, if that voice belonged to Rachel McCarthy. He wanted a chance to look around before he met the woman who owned the other half of this business.

Matthew aimed a sharp, appraising gaze over the vast room. First to catch his notice were the filled bookcases that lined a long, tall, pink wall. Oh, yes, he'd expected them, and there they were: Romances with muscular men and beautiful women on the covers. All too predictable, he thought. But when he shifted his gaze to a far corner of the room, one black eyebrow lifted in surprise. *Well, I'll be a—*

"Can I help you?" a soft voice asked, this time from almost beside him.

"What's that...thing doing in here?" he asked, still looking at the latticed white wicker sides of the object gripping his attention.

"It's a gazebo," the voice explained patiently. "It provides a place for people to sit and have a cup of our coffee, if they like. What do you think of it?"

Matthew frowned. "Doesn't it belong outside?"

The low chuckle that followed wasn't the delicate sound he would have expected from the softness of her voice. It was a deep, bordering on sultry laugh. He turned to look at the woman who stood next to him.

She wasn't quite what he'd expected, either. If she *was* Rachel McCarthy, he knew she was twenty-nine and a widow—the lawyer had provided that information—but she looked younger, maybe because her long hair, a medium shade of brown, was caught up in a ponytail like a teenager's. *Medium* would also describe her height; the top of her head was nearly level with his chin. Her nose was too short for true beauty, her mouth a little too wide. Still, she was attractive in a pleasing, a-bit-above-average way.

Except for her eyes.

They were anything *but* average.

A provocative, luminous green, they tilted up at the outside corners rather exotically. Bedroom eyes...to go with the sensual laugh. They made him think of steamy nights that owed nothing to the temperature. But *her* thoughts clearly didn't coincide with his; she merely continued to smile up at him in a relaxed, friendly manner, although there was a hint of puzzlement in her expression.

"If the gazebo was outside," she said, "people wouldn't recall it as well. This way, we're 'that store with the gazebo inside.' People remember and tell others about us. It's good advertising."

"Well, I guess that makes some sort of sense." *In a crazy kind of way,* he thought.

If his less-than-enthusiastic statement didn't please her, it wasn't apparent. "Can I help you?" she repeated calmly.

"You can if you're Rachel McCarthy." She nodded in reply. "My aunt's lawyer, Benjamin Bradford, said he'd called to tell you I would be here." With that, he saw her expression suddenly turn cautious...wary. "I'm Matthew Kent."

Rachel took a deep breath. *That's why he seems so familiar,* she thought. It was the McCarthy in him. She should have immediately recognized those swarthy good looks combined with a tall, lean frame, so much like the rest of the McCarthys...so much like her late husband, his cousin.

"Yes, I was expecting you sometime later this week, Mr. Kent," she said with all the casualness she could summon as she extended her hand in a businesslike fashion. The instant their palms met she fought an urge to pull back as a jolt of something unrecognizable pulsed through her. Somehow it was much too intimate, touching this man even for a brief moment. "I'm pleased to meet you," she added, though she wasn't at all sure it was true.

"I was able to come a couple of days earlier than I initially planned. I'm glad to meet you, Mrs.—Ms.?" He hesitated over the title, probably more for politeness' sake than because he was unsure. He looked like a man who was always sure of himself, Rachel reflected. In fact, in his well-tailored navy wool suit, crisp white shirt, striped tie and highly polished wing tips, he exuded confidence.

"Rachel's fine," she replied, all at once feeling a trifle grubby in her faded jeans, oversize T-shirt and canvas shoes.

"And I'm Matthew, please."

Then that handshake was completed and Rachel was relieved, yet somewhat concerned about her reaction to his touch. If she had to spend time with this man, how would she cope? She might have felt easier, more reassured, if his eyes had been the same warm brown as most of the McCarthy clan. But his eyes weren't brown or warm; they were as silver-gray as stainless steel and seemed to pierce straight through her skin, right to the heart of her.

"This is quite a place you have here," he said.

She caught the underlying disdain is his low voice, although he'd spoken courteously enough. Normally it wouldn't have bothered her; she was used to the occasional cynical remark regarding the store's concept, especially from male visitors who had plainly been dragged in by the women in their lives.

This man, however, was no mere visitor. Soon he might inherit his aunt's share of the business.

She squared her shoulders. "You'll find it's quite a profitable place, Mr.—Matthew. Jerome may not be a very large city, but with Sedona and Oak Creek Canyon nearby, thousands of people visit every year. The store's doing fairly well even now, in August, which is our slowest month. When tourists return to Arizona in full force in the winter, it becomes very lucrative, for a small operation. Some people—a lot of people—believe in romance," she added coolly, lifting her chin.

"Do *you?*" It was a blunt question.

"Absolutely." It was as emphatic a statement as she could make it.

His firm mouth curved faintly, imperturbably...maddeningly. "Then I guess you're the ideal person to show me around."

Suddenly she longed to stomp an old canvas shoe on his toes, covered by burnished Italian leather. Oh, yes. She'd love to do that. And couldn't. Like it or not, she *had* to show him around.

THEY BEGAN WITH a cup of coffee.

Matthew sat at one of the small, round tables inside the gazebo and watched as Rachel walked over to a coffeemaker set at the rear, noting the graceful movement of her body. She was neither model-thin nor voluptuously curvy, he observed, yet the fluid sway of supple hips encased in snug-fitting denim definitely proclaimed her a female—though a female clearly not thrilled with his presence. Well, he wasn't thrilled to be here, either.

Still, he welcomed the rich smell of the coffee she poured from a glass carafe as he stretched his long legs out to the side. He needed the caffeine; his internal clock still hadn't totally adjusted to being back in the United States.

"Cream or sugar?"

"No, just black is fine."

She returned and handed him a large white mug trimmed with tiny gold figures. He winced; he couldn't help it. "Cupids?"

She tapped a foot irritably on the slatted wood floor. "Do you have a problem with that?"

If he said yes, she'd probably snatch the mug back and dump the contents in his lap. So he merely took a long swallow. Although the container was entirely too cute for his taste, he had no quarrel with the coffee itself. It was delicious, and he told her so.

She set a matching mug down and moved to the chair across from him. "It's so nice to know *something* around here is to your liking," she said with patently false gratitude.

Matthew was debating whether or not to respond to that when the front door opened. The woman who entered was forty-something with a head of short, strawberry-red hair topping a petite body. Rachel's quick grin told him she was happy to see the new arrival. It was different, brighter and warmer, than the professionally welcoming smile she'd given him on his arrival—her storekeeper's smile.

"Excuse me," she said, before turning away and walking toward the front counter. "Hi, Darlene. How are you?"

"Just fine," the redhead replied. "I wanted to tell you I finished the book you recommended. It was great."

"Glad you liked it. How's business at the candy store?"

"Can't complain. Ron and I are holding our own. There's one comforting fact about chocolate—it's addictive. People have to have it, no matter what time of year. But I'm not here to talk about business," she added slyly. "I've got other things on my mind. Has that new book with Dirk Dahlstrom on the cover come in?"

"Uh-huh. I've got your copy right here." Rachel reached under the counter and pulled out a thick paperback. She handed it to the other woman.

The redhead took one long look and sighed. "That man can certainly rev up my engine anytime he'd like—" she winked suggestively "—if you get my meaning."

Rachel pursed her lips. "Your husband would take serious objection to that procedure, I'm sure."

"You're right. Ron got a tad testy yesterday when a handsome salesman at the shoe store in Cottonwood was so enthusiastic about helping me try on some high heels."

Darlene was clearly pleased by that fact. "And speaking of the green-eyed monster, *I'll* be the jealous one if you win that evening with the devastating Mr. Dahlstrom. You *did* enter?"

"The contest for independent bookstore owners? I think Bonnie filled out the form and sent it in. I've never won anything in my life, but Bonnie had a *feeling*."

The women exchanged a knowing look. Darlene smiled. "You'll thank her if you wind up on Dirk Dahlstrom's arm. He might even rev up *your* engine."

"Oh, yeah, sure," Rachel kidded. "That'll be right around the time Atlantis rises from the ocean."

Both women laughed, and the redhead left with the newly purchased book in hand.

Rachel returned to Matthew.

"After that conversation, I can't help but wonder about the 'devastating Mr. Dahlstrom,'" he admitted.

She picked up her mug and took a short swallow. "He's the male model who's creating quite a stir as the hero depicted on the covers of several recent romance novels."

"And that particular accomplishment makes him so desirable?"

Her nod was decisive. "It certainly does—to a *lot* of women. If you're ready for a look around, we can start with the book area. I'll show you the man in question."

Moments later, Matthew stood in front of one of the tall bookcases, looking at a novel cover featuring a bare-chested, brawny blond male with shoulder-length hair. A sinewy arm, biceps bulging, was clamped around a raven-haired beauty.

"That's Dirk Dahlstrom," Rachel informed him. "His popularity has been a tremendous asset to the industry. It's helped sell a great deal of books."

"Hmmm. A little muscle-bound, isn't he?"

"Oh, I don't know. That broad, tanned chest and those pectorals are quite a sight."

"I have to admit you're right on that score. He's got nearly as much cleavage as *she* has," Matthew said dryly, his last words a reference to the well-endowed heroine. Then, before he consciously considered it, he turned his head and dropped a fleeting glance toward Rachel's chest. He found himself wondering about her breasts, which were loosely covered by a pink cotton knit embellished with a blue logo that proclaimed Caring Is In—Try It, You'll Like It! To his amazement, just that brief moment of speculation generated a sensation that was more erotic than anything he'd felt for some time.

What the devil is the matter with you, Kent? he asked himself as he turned back to the bookcase and shoved the paperback into an empty slot with more force than was strictly necessary. It had been a very long time—if ever—since he'd had that kind of reaction to a female, and the realization didn't please him. She was all wrong for him, he told himself.

Rachel McCarthy wasn't his kind of woman.

Any female who championed this type of business would not be his kind of woman—even one with bedroom eyes.

Rachel ran her tongue over her lips. She'd been instantly aware of the way Matthew's gaze had crossed her breasts and had resisted the urge to fold her arms in front of her, but she couldn't halt the thoughts that still raced through her mind while she watched his silent perusal of the remaining contents of the bookshelves.

Had she imagined it? His look, though intent, had come and gone very quickly. And even if she hadn't imagined it, it was probably more curiosity than anything. She knew her body would provide little competition to the gorgeous women so vividly displayed on these novel covers. A femme fatale she wasn't. Still, she couldn't shake the tension—the heightened awareness—he'd created inside her, even when he began to display a sharp intelligence and undeniable business acumen by asking shrewd, pointed questions about the store's dealings with the publishing industry. She had to rally her thoughts in an effort to answer calmly and succinctly.

Before long, they left the books and moved on to the store's other merchandise. "Potpourri in various scents is a big seller these days," she said, waving a hand toward a large oak table that held an assortment of bags. "Fortunately there's a woman right here in Jerome who makes it. She dries the flowers and adds oils to deepen the scent—maybe some spices, too, depending on the blend."

Matthew nodded as they approached the table. "So you can get the product directly from the source and cut out the distributor. That has to increase the profit margin substantially."

"And we get to choose the names of the different blends," Rachel added proudly. "It makes them unique to this store."

Matthew picked up one of the clear cellophane bags topped with a bright silver ribbon and read the glossy label. "I see there's Lavender For Lovers—" he put it down and retrieved another "—and Forbidden Fantasy Floral."

"That's the scent we have in small containers scattered around the store."

As he replaced the package, his gaze skimmed over the rest of the bags. Then, one eyebrow cocked, he looked at Rachel. "What's this, no Rev-Up-Your-Engine Rose?"

Surprised, Rachel laughed. A moment ago she wouldn't have bet two cents that this man had a keen, though dry, sense of humor under all that self-assurance. Yet he obviously did. "I'll be sure to pass your suggestion on to Bonnie Gallico," she said with mock gravity. "Besides working here several days a week, Bonnie's the creative force behind most of our potpourri titles.''

"And the woman with the *feeling*," he added.

So he'd caught that exchange with Darlene. The man was perceptive as well as intelligent. Before Rachel could respond, the bell chimed as a customer entered. "Sorry, you'll have to excuse me. Our 'lotion and potion' collection is the next stop—along that far wall."

She returned minutes later and discovered Matthew studying the variety of bath and cosmetic items residing in a huge oak cabinet. "We try to stock whatever's not usually found in drugstores," she told him. "And it's all environmentally correct, which is becoming very important."

He plucked a bottle of creamy liquid from a shelf and read the label. "Hands of Love?"

"It's the brand name of a line of massage oils and lotions."

"Hmmm." He replaced the bottle and moved his gaze along the shelf to a wicker basket filled with small white packets bordered in gold. "I don't believe it," he muttered. "Pixie Dust?"

"It's actually a micro-fine, iridescent power that can be sprinkled on pillows, or anywhere else for that matter. It's a bit of whimsy."

"Why in the world would anyone buy something so totally useless?"

Rachel lifted one shoulder in a slight shrug. "I can only tell you it makes a good extra to add to a larger present, and it can even be used as a stocking stuffer. We sold nearly three hundred of those *'useless'* packets last Christmas."

"*Three hundred.*" He mulled that over, but for only an instant. "What's the markup percentage?"

Barely suppressing another startled laugh at his swift shift from astonishment to economics, she answered his question and discussed sales trends as they walked on, continuing to make a wide circle around the room. "Our greeting cards and wrapping paper are always good sellers, but especially at Christmas and Valentine's Day. We sell a lot of candles, too."

The tour progressed past a display of compact discs featuring love songs and mood music, a small collection of movies that were essentially love stories, some glass cases containing inexpensive jewelry, and a long brass rack holding a variety of T-shirts.

It was going better than she'd expected, Rachel decided. Matthew Kent seemed to have forgotten—or at least put aside for the moment—his initial displeasure with the fact that this operation's central theme was romance. Now, because he was viewing it purely from a business angle, she felt she could lower her defenses. Now she could vanquish the lingering tension that had kept her on edge. Now she could relax.

And she did.

Right up to the moment they reached the last section.

Lingerie.

HIS MIND INTENT on the imaginary balance sheet he was envisioning, Matthew opened his mouth to voice a question on overhead expenses—only to snap it closed, stopping dead in his tracks when his eyes connected with an object displayed on a plumply padded hanger directly in front of him.

He knew it was one of those skimpy creations sometimes called a "merry widow," but every male past puberty knew its real name: sex. Slowly he moved his gaze downward over the garment, starting with the ruffle-edged strapless top, past airily woven black lace that would reveal rather than conceal a woman's breasts and torso, to long black garters tipped by tiny white satin roses.

Normally he would have made a flippant comment and dismissed it. But obviously today wasn't a normal day, Matthew concluded, because his mouth had gone bone-dry—and it had nothing to do with thirst. And undoubtedly everything to do with the woman who'd come to a halt beside him.

Clearing his throat to ease a sudden tightness, he slanted a glance her way and found those stunning green eyes staring at him before she caught his look and dropped her gaze to the floor. He could sense her discomfort, yet he couldn't stop himself from imagining how she would look in see-through lace, long silk stockings, very high heels—and nothing else. In a heartbeat, his body started to respond.

Damn. He'd always controlled his libido as effectively as he controlled everything else in his life. Until now.

"I take it this is the 'intimate apparel' area," he muttered, his voice husky despite his efforts to master his reaction.

"Yes," Rachel murmured. She lifted her eyes but avoided his by turning to look straight ahead. He noticed that she quickly braced her shoulders as she walked forward. Uncomfortable as she clearly was, her voice was calm and steady when she spoke. "This is one of our most popular sections, second only to books in sales."

Following her, Matthew glanced at the selection of feminine nightwear, bras and panties—a profusion of silk, satin and lace—displayed on several tables and a long wooden rack. There were also brightly patterned briefs and silk boxer shorts for men.

"Well, you certainly have an assortment," was the sole comment he could muster. Then he spied several small pink-and-brown boxes resting on a table next to the panties. Intrigued in spite of himself, he moved closer. "What are these?"

This time Rachel's voice faltered. "They're...ah...edible underwear."

For a moment he didn't get it. "Edible?" he asked, shooting her a quizzical look.

"Strawberry for women...and chocolate for men."

"You mean you can eat—" All at once awareness zinged through him, and he realized what a man was supposed to do to a woman who wore edible underwear. And vice versa. "I see," he managed to force out after several seconds of utter silence.

Matthew told himself he had to leave. Now. Before he did something truly inexcusable. Like grabbing Rachel McCarthy and kissing the hell out of her.

Something was definitely wrong with him.

With the hope that he didn't look as perturbed as he felt, he gritted his teeth and walked resolutely ahead until he found himself back at the book section. "It seems we've completed the tour of the store," he said, grateful for the level tone that had reentered his voice. "Thanks for showing me around. I have a reservation at a hotel in Flagstaff, so I'll be going now."

He saw his guide's composure return, accompanied by bewilderment. "You don't want to see the rest of the house? The lawyer asked me to show you everything, so that when the will was read you'd have a better idea of the property involved."

"I think I've taken up enough of your time," he replied as he started for the door. He knew he was being abrupt and that it would be courteous to shake hands again, at least. But he couldn't risk touching her. He turned to face her only when his long fingers made contact with the door handle. "Bradford would like to read the will tomorrow morning at eleven o'clock in his office. He wanted me to ask if that's convenient for you."

She blinked in surprise. "He wants *me* to be there?"

Matthew nodded, just once. "He indicated my aunt had requested it. He also asked me to find out if her brother Jackson could attend. Bradford told me McCarthy's sometimes a difficult man to reach, but that you might know his whereabouts."

Rachel walked forward until she was a few feet away from the man poised to leave. "I'll be glad to come. Jack, however, is off 'communicating with nature' as he calls it. He's in a tent somewhere in the White Mountains." Her mouth curved in a faint smile as she thought of Jackson McCarthy, her late husband's uncle. He was one of her favorite people, even if she did get an occasional urge to strangle him for his complete lack of diplomacy. "When Jack left, he said he'd see me in a week...or a month. Time doesn't mean much to him. He's not exactly fond of lawyers either, as Benjamin Bradford probably well knows, since he and Jack have encountered each other over the years. Jack's never been reticent about expressing his opinions. Tomorrow's meeting will likely go more smoothly—and certainly more peacefully—without him."

"All right," Matthew agreed. "I'll see you at the lawyer's office in Flagstaff."

But Rachel, though heartily relieved by his imminent departure, felt she couldn't let him go without saying something more. The McCarthys were, after all, his family, although she knew he'd had no contact with them for many years. "About your aunt, I'm sorry, Matthew. I tried to reach you to tell you about the funeral arrangements, but your assistant said you were in Japan." She paused. "Although Ava never complained—her philosophy was that it was better to laugh at adversity than gripe about it—it was obvious she hadn't been feeling really well for some time, and then her health took a serious turn for the worse. Ever since Luther died, she—" Rachel stopped as a thought occurred to her. "Did you know she had been married to a local artist, Luther LaMont?"

He nodded. "The lawyer told me. He was husband number four—after the tennis player, the dance instructor and the jazz musician—wasn't he?"

Though it took some effort, Rachel ignored the irony in his voice. "Ava was divorced three times before she met Luther," she acknowledged. "But she once said she'd merely been practicing until the real love of her life came along. And they were truly in love. No one who saw them together could doubt that."

Matthew Kent doubted it. She could see it plainly written in his stony expression. "I liked them both very much," she added somewhat defiantly.

"I'm sure you did," he assured her, his mouth twitching in that imperturbable, maddening way.

She had the urge to stomp on those toes again. "And they *were* in love," she felt compelled to say. "I've already figured out that you don't believe in romance, but—"

"I don't believe in love either, Rachel." With that brusque statement, uttered with a stark look in his gray eyes that told her he'd meant every word, he opened the door and walked out.

Rachel moved to the window and peered through bright sunshine to watch a black Lexus sedan pull away.

Matthew Kent was gone. For now.

I DON'T BELIEVE in love either, Rachel.

Rachel pondered that statement as she lay in bed that night in the large apartment occupying the entire third floor of the house. If Matthew Kent became her partner, she thought, it would probably be a disaster of epic proportions.

Not that he wasn't a good businessman.

From Benjamin Bradford and the business section of the newspaper, Rachel had learned that Matthew was thirty-six years old, unmarried, had become president and CEO of Kent Enterprises upon his father's death two years earlier, and lived in Denver, where his company was headquartered. Matthew's recent trip to the Orient had included the sale of Kent Enterprises' holdings in the Far East, for which he purportedly received a very generous sum. Speculation now flourished among members of the business community that Matthew Kent was in the process of downsizing his company's various interests; if so, it would be a radical departure from his late father's expansion goals.

From Ava LaMont, Rachel had found out that Matthew was an only child who had been raised by his father after Ava's younger sister, Rosalind Kent, had died when Matthew was four years old. Ava herself had not been able to have children—one of the few regrets she'd had about a life she had lived as she'd wanted to, not as other people might have considered "proper."

Another regret related to her nephew Matthew. "I wish I had had the chance to get to know Matt," Ava had once told Rachel. "But after Rosalind was gone, Andrew firmly discouraged any contact with our side of the family. Probably thought the 'crazy' McCarthys would taint his only son."

From her meeting with Matthew today, Rachel had discovered that there was something disturbingly different about the man with the steel-gray eyes. At least he affected her differently than any man she had ever encountered.

She couldn't forget the episode in the lingerie section. Even more surprising than his unexpected reaction to the intimate wear—she didn't believe for one second that the coolly self-assured man was that easily flustered—was her unprecedented response. She was accustomed to helping people make intimate purchases, both for themselves and as gifts. There had been times when customers, especially some of the men, had clearly been uncomfortable buying lingerie, and she'd always done her best to put them at ease by acting as impersonally as possible—just as though they were buying flannel pajamas for their grandmothers. It had never been a problem. Until today.

Matthew Kent had made it seem all too personal.

Her response to him had been all too personal.

Tomorrow, they would hear the terms of Ava's will. In accordance with Ava's instructions, the only information the lawyer had released so far was that, except for a few minor bequests, Ava had left her entire estate, including her half interest in the Realm of Romance, to her nephew—provided he was willing to comply with certain conditions.

What would they be? Rachel wondered for the umpteenth time. She shifted restlessly, seeking a comfortable position that refused to be found.

Sleep was going to elude her, she concluded an hour later, staring up at the ceiling. Even the placid night sounds of Mingus Mountain, carried on a soft breeze that stirred the lacy curtains framing the open windows, sounds normally so soothing to her, didn't seem to help tonight.

"You should go downstairs and balance the books for last month, Rach," she told herself with a rueful grimace. Although bookkeeping was by no means her favorite pastime, it was a necessary chore. Yes, she should do that.

But she wasn't going to.

Because she couldn't stop herself from imagining the disaster of epic proportions that was bound to occur if a man who didn't believe in romance—or love—became her partner.

2

"If it's acceptable to you, I'll dispense with reading the document and merely relate the provisions of your aunt's will."

"All right," Matthew agreed, grateful to be spared the "whereases" and "wherefores." When it came to business, he preferred to deal with people who spoke his language. Apparently Benjamin Bradford, a dignified, silver-haired man who seemed as shrewdly intelligent as he was briskly professional, had recognized that and decided to proceed in a forthright manner.

While the lawyer assembled his papers, Matthew slid a glance at the woman seated beside him. Yesterday, Rachel McCarthy had looked younger than her twenty-nine years in her casual clothes. Today, she looked closer to her age, dressed like the consummate businesswoman in a beige linen suit and cream-colored blouse, her long hair bound in an upswept style. Yesterday, she'd worn no makeup; today, she did, although it was lightly applied. And yesterday, he hadn't been able to see—really see—her legs, since she'd worn jeans. Today, he could see those legs. Softly curved, encased in silky panty hose, and complemented by beige mid-heeled pumps, he had to admit they were a very pleasurable sight.

But he had an iron clamp on his thoughts today.

There would be no repetition of yesterday's events.

"Ahem." Bradford cleared his throat and began to speak. "First of all, let me state that this will was signed by Ava LaMont six months prior to her death. I would like to add that, while her physical health seemed to be failing, Ava was in complete command of her mental faculties at that time, and as alert, cheerful and intelligent as I'd always found her to be.''

What the devil is he leading up to? Matthew angled another glance at Rachel. She appeared to be as puzzled as he was.

''As to the basic provisions of the will,'' the attorney continued, ''to her brother, Raymond McCarthy, and his wife, Marla McCarthy, both now residing in San Diego, California, Ava has given her late husband's entire collection of antique spittoons.''

Rachel's laugh, soft and muffled, had Bradford aiming a quelling stare at her over the top of his gold-rimmed glasses. ''Sorry,'' she murmured, although her expression remained amused. ''It's just that, while I had a good relationship with Ray and Marla—I couldn't have asked for nicer in-laws—Marla and Ava never exactly saw eye to eye. Ray always admired Luther's collection, but Marla made no secret of the fact that she considered those old spittoons to be somewhat tacky. I wondered why you asked me to have them packed. I'd love to see the expression on Marla's face when they arrive on her doorstep...all five cartons full.''

''Yes, well, be that as it may,'' the lawyer said, forging on, ''we now come to the second bequest. To her brother, Jackson McCarthy, Ava has given five acres of land adjoining the property on which her cabin is located. Apparently Jackson has already erected a small dwelling on this acreage.'' From his ironic tone, Bradford was visualizing something closer to a shack when he'd referred to a dwelling. ''Ava has left nothing else to Jackson. She states as part of this provision that her brother Jack is the only person she knows who has everything he wants and needs in life, and she's happy to leave him in that condition.''

Again Rachel laughed softly, but this time the attorney joined in as he turned his attention to her. ''Ava had quite a sense of humor, and it was obvious to anyone who saw the two of you together that you enjoyed the relationship you had. So I'm very pleased to say that the third provision of Ava's will relates to a bequest to her niece by marriage, business associate and friend, Rachel Wilson McCarthy. Ava has given you a Luther LaMont painting titled *Sunrise and Red Rocks.*''

Rachel's expression sobered. ''Ava knew that was my favorite. I'll cherish it.''

As Bradford shifted his gaze to Matthew, his professional demeanor returned abruptly. ''And now we come to the final provision of the will. Other than clothing and other personal effects, which have been donated to a women's shelter, Ava LaMont has bequeathed her entire estate to her nephew, Matthew Kent, provided he is willing to comply with certain conditions. This estate consists of her half interest in the business she and Rachel McCarthy founded, the house in Jerome that is also the site of that business, and her cabin and twenty acres of land located on Mingus Mountain. In addition, there are various bank accounts, stocks and bonds which add up to a considerable sum.''

The total amount the lawyer named startled Matthew. His aunt had been a moderately wealthy woman.

Clearly noting his surprised expression, Bradford smiled faintly. ''As I stated earlier, Ava LaMont was an intelligent woman. She was also a shrewd investor. Most of the funds now part of the estate originated with profits from paintings Luther LaMont sold prior to his death, but it was Ava who made the investments that more than doubled that money.''

''I had no idea....'' Matthew began, then fell silent.

''Neither did I,'' he heard Rachel whisper softly.

"I don't believe many people did, Mr. Kent," the attorney said. "When Ava wanted to, she could be a very private person.

"Now, regarding the conditions which must be met, there are two. The first requires you to spend six consecutive weeks in Jerome, Arizona, residing on a day-to-day basis in your aunt's house, with the exception that up to two weeks of this period may be spent at her cabin, or other areas in a hundred-mile radius of Jerome. Do you have any questions regarding that?"

With a quick shake of his head that evidenced his sudden impatience to have everything out in the open, Matthew replied, "It seems to be crystal clear. And the second condition?"

"That during this six-week period you will not participate in any matters whatsoever relating to Kent Enterprises or any of its holdings, which would include telephone calls, fax transmissions, written correspondence, and visits to and from associates pertaining to business dealings."

Benjamin Bradford laid down his papers and folded his arms. "In other words, your aunt wanted you to take a vacation."

Complete silence reigned while Matthew considered what the lawyer had just told him.

This is so ridiculous, you should just get up and walk out, Kent. He didn't want or need a vacation. He'd taken vacations before, and they had always been a great deal more trouble than they were worth. Work had piled up in spite of the fact that he'd been in constant contact with his office. And now he was supposed to leave for six weeks and have no contact whatsoever?

It was unthinkable.

He also didn't need his aunt's property or her money. He had plenty of his own. And he certainly didn't need to be in the romance business. What a joke that would be! If any members of the numerous boards of directors on which he sat heard about it, they'd laugh their heads off. He had to put a stop to this nonsense here and now, he decided. Someone else could have Ava LaMont's estate—and be welcome to it.

He'd opened his mouth to say exactly that when Bradford spoke again. "Before you make a decision, I believe it's only fair you know what will happen to the estate if you decline."

Matthew sighed gustily, more impatient than ever. "All right, let's get on with it."

Bradford retrieved his papers. "Your aunt has stipulated that, should you choose not to accept her conditions, her entire estate will become part of a beneficial trust, which would be initiated in accordance with the terms of a document she executed on the same day she signed her will. This trust would be established for—and I quote her exact words—'a great companion and faithful friend, my wonderful Hodgepodge.'"

Matthew heard Rachel's gasp as he speared the lawyer with a penetrating stare. "Who the devil is *Hodgepodge?*"

Bradford shifted in his brown leather chair and squared the shoulders beneath his dark blue suit, all at once taking on the appearance of a man braced for disaster.

"Hodgepodge is your aunt's dog."

Instantly all hell broke loose.

Rachel watched as Matthew shot to his feet, shoving his chair back with enough force to send it sliding across the room. It crashed resoundingly against the wall. "That's crazy! *She'd leave all that to a damn dog?*"

Slowly, looking as if nothing unusual had happened, the lawyer rose and faced Matthew. "Only if *you* choose not to accept it, Mr. Kent," he calmly reminded him.

Matthew emitted a low, succinct curse, then spun around on his heel and began to stalk back and forth across the office with quick, even strides of his long legs. Although he was again dressed like a polished, conservative businessman in his light gray suit, white shirt and paisley tie, Rachel decided there was nothing polished about his expression. Not now. Now, he looked more than a little uncivilized. Even…primitive. Matthew Kent was not a man to cross. That was quite obvious.

And he had a temper.

Rachel wondered what she would do if all that anger were directed at her. She had no idea of the answer, since she'd never had to deal with anyone as volatile as the furious male who was pacing the room like an edgy panther.

"Did my aunt really expect me to agree to those conditions?" he snapped, not even slowing his steps. "And then to choose a mongrel as an alternate! What was she thinking? Or *was* she thinking?" He didn't seem to require a response, got none, and continued his one-way conversation, muttering under his breath. Every now and then a reference to "flighty McCarthys" could be heard.

Rachel ventured a look at the lawyer and saw a small, satisfied smile curl the dignified man's thin lips. It came and went very quickly—yet not quickly enough to escape her notice. Benjamin Bradford was pleased about something, she concluded. And he clearly didn't wish to broadcast that fact, because his expression was once again impassive as Matthew came to a stop in front of the desk and turned to look at him.

"I could take this to court," Matthew said, his voice suddenly far too soft. Somehow it sounded more fierce than his earlier shouting.

The attorney nodded agreeably. "And we could spend some considerable time there—time, effort and money. As executor, I would be forced to defend your aunt's will, using a portion of the estate's funds. Is that what you really want?"

"No, that's not what I want," Matthew said through his teeth. "But I won't—can't—stand by and see it all go to a *dog,* for God's sake. I have too much respect for money and the hard work involved in acquiring it."

"Then is six weeks of your time too much to ask to secure the estate? Once it's yours, you can deal with it as you choose. I realize you don't need the money, but it could be used for some good causes. And, if I may say so, Rachel could benefit from your involvement in the store's operation. You have a wealth of business experience, and I believe she would be grateful for the chance to learn from you. Wouldn't you, Rachel?"

Caught off guard, Rachel was momentarily rendered mute. She was supposed to spend six weeks with Matthew Kent? *Six weeks!* She sat absolutely still, not even blinking an eye, as she thought about what that would mean—being with him, working with him, *living in the same house with him.* Then, realizing she'd delayed her reply too long for good manners, she tried for diplomacy. "Yes, well, while I would welcome the benefit of Mr. Kent's experience, of course, I couldn't impose on him." Hesitantly she moved her gaze to look directly into his steel-gray eyes. "Besides, I'm sure you would have other things to occupy—"

"But I wouldn't," Matthew broke in bluntly. "I wouldn't have *anything* else to occupy me."

"Don't you have any hobbies?" she asked with a hint of desperation.

"No."

His concise reply spoke volumes to Rachel. It was a telling indication of a personality type once heartbreakingly familiar to her. Matthew Kent obviously had little time in his life for anything except business, just like—

Bradford's smooth voice penetrated her thoughts. "Does that mean you're considering an agreement to the conditions of the will, Mr. Kent?"

Although Matthew's jaw tightened visibly as he again faced the attorney, there was no repeat of the earlier outburst. "It seems so," he conceded, "since there appears to be no viable alternative. And I've found there's seldom an advantage to be gained by delaying the inevitable. In this case, since it's now the beginning of August and summer would be the best—scratch that, *a marginally better*—time for me to be away, I'll be back in Jerome next Monday to begin the six-week period. I don't like it, but I'll be there," he concluded with a deep frown.

Just that swiftly he had made up his mind. It told Rachel something else about Matthew Kent: he was a man of action.

Rachel eyed Benjamin Bradford closely, looking for some sign of his reaction to Matthew's decision, and saw nothing more than polite acknowledgement. "I'm sure everything will work out," he said encouragingly.

"Will someone be appointed to play guardian and verify that I observe the conditions?"

The lawyer ignored the sarcasm in that question. "Not at all. No provision was made for verification, since your aunt was positive that if you agreed, you would abide by the conditions. I remember our discussion on that subject, and the remark she made that the McCarthys always kept their word."

"I'm not a Mc—" Matthew started to say, before abruptly clamping his mouth shut.

Yes, he *was* a McCarthy—half McCarthy, at any rate— and he couldn't deny it, Rachel thought. She had no idea why, but all at once she was certain that Ava had, through the terms of her astonishing will, issued a challenge to her nephew. And he'd just accepted it.

THIRTY MINUTES LATER Matthew was coming to his own conclusions as he opened the door to a small roadside res-

taurant and let Rachel precede him into a room bordered
by red vinyl booths. The white Formica tabletops sparkled,
reflecting the midday sunshine that streamed in through the
wide, plate-glass windows. Wafting in from the kitchen
area was the aroma of potatoes frying in hot oil.

Ever since leaving the lawyer's office, Matthew had had
the distinct, unwelcome feeling he'd been manipulated at
that meeting. It was a unique sensation. If anyone had gotten the better of him in the past, it was so long ago he
couldn't remember. His father had raised him to deal with
life on a rational basis. ''Feelings are a luxury one can't
afford in business,'' had been one of Andrew Kent's max-
ims.

And that had been the problem, Matthew decided as he
followed Rachel past a string of swivel stools lining a long
counter. He had let emotion into the equation—''flagrant
McCarthy emotionalism,'' his father would have termed
it—when he'd lost his temper during the reading of the will.
These days, that was an extremely rare occurrence. Oh, he
had a temper—had always had one—yet it had been years
since he'd totally lost it. It wasn't at all typical of him. But
then, he thought ruefully, nothing about this visit to Arizona
had been typical, including his first meeting with the
woman who had agreed, with perceptible reluctance, to
have lunch with him.

Rachel stopped beside an empty corner booth. A tray of
condiments and some small menus rested against the wood-
paneled wall. ''Is this okay with you?''

Matthew nodded, and they slid into seats on opposite
sides of the booth, facing each other. ''Do you come here
often?'' he asked. Rachel had suggested the restaurant,
which was only a ten-minute drive from Benjamin Bradford's office. They'd decided to use Matthew's Lexus; he'd
return Rachel to her car.

''I used to eat here quite a bit when I was going to

college in Flagstaff. Northern Arizona University is fairly close by. But I haven't been to Harold's Hamburger Heaven for a long time—or at least it seems like a long time. Maybe it's just that my life is so different now, so many things have changed.''

He wanted to probe deeper, learn more about her, but a plump, sixtyish woman in waitress attire was bustling toward the booth. She also wore a broad smile on her bright orange lips, which were almost the same shade as her short, curly hair.

''Rachel, honey, it's about time you paid us a visit!''

Suddenly grinning, Rachel said, ''It's good to be here, Arlene. How's your husband?''

''Harold's an old man with young ideas, same as usual,'' Arlene joked. ''Things going okay at the store?''

''They're fine.'' Rachel's green eyes took on an impish spark. ''We got a new shipment in of those, ah, items you like.''

After a quick glance at Matthew, Arlene dropped her gaze to study the order pad she held in a surprisingly elegant hand. ''Well, I guess I'll have to get over to Jerome this week and take a look at those…items. Now, what'll you folks have?''

''Are Harold's burgers just as good as they used to be?''

''Course they are, honey.''

Rachel looked at Matthew. ''Then I can confidently recommend the cheeseburger-plate special.''

''All right,'' he agreed. ''Make it two specials and two…?''

''Double chocolate malts?'' Rachel ventured.

Matthew winced and turned to the waitress. ''Make that one malt and one iced tea, please.''

Arlene gave him another look, this one edged with speculation, then left to fill their order. Someone fed the jukebox nearby, choosing a rock-and-roll tune.

"Dare I ask what those intriguingly undisclosed *items* are?" he asked in a mock whisper.

"My lips are sealed," Rachel said, her eyes sparkling.

And what nice lips you have, thought Matthew, before giving himself a mental kick. He had no business admiring her lips. "Are you originally from this area?" he asked, pursuing his resolve to find out more about her.

She shook her head. "I was born and raised in southeastern Arizona, on the outskirts of Tucson. My parents and younger brother still live there."

"And you chose to stay in the northern part of the state after you finished college?"

"Uh-huh. I was an English Lit major and was lucky enough to obtain a position at a library here in Flagstaff. After Danny got his pilot's license, he worked for a small airline that flies groups of sightseers over the Grand Canyon area." She lowered her eyes to look at her hands, laced together and resting on the table. "Daniel McCarthy was my husband. His dream was to be a pilot for one of the major airlines."

"Bradford told me your husband and Luther LaMont were killed three years ago transporting a shipment of LaMont's paintings to Phoenix for a show at one of the galleries. He said the plane they chartered went down in a storm." Matthew had decided to add that statement to spare her an explanation. "I'm very sorry, Rachel," he said with complete sincerity. Though he had never met his cousin, any young person's death was a tragedy.

"Thank you," she said softly, once again looking at him, her expression serene.

She had accepted her husband's death, Matthew concluded, and that harsh lesson in reality didn't seem to have disillusioned her. No doubt she was still an optimist; she might even still believe in happily-ever-after. She had, after all, informed him yesterday—quite emphatically—that she believed in romance.

The recollection prompted him to ask, "How did you make the transition from a library in Flagstaff to a store in Jerome?"

Rachel crossed her arms and leaned forward. "The store was actually an idea I'd had in the back of my mind for some time. Danny and I were already engaged when we came up from Tucson to enter N.A.U., and we began to see quite a bit of his Aunt Ava and her husband, since they lived nearby. Back then, they were dividing their time between the cabin and the house in Jerome, where Luther had his studio.

"One day I mentioned the concept for the store while the four of us were together. The men were immediately skeptical of the premise that romance could support a business—which I'm beginning to believe is an inherently male view." Matthew recognized that as a right-on-target reference to *his* attitude. "Ava, however, being an intelligent *woman*—" Rachel emphasized that word with a wry look "—was enthusiastic. Still, it remained something she and I merely talked about...until almost a year after we lost Danny and Luther."

Just then Arlene brought their order. Matthew's eyes widened at the sight of the huge cheeseburger, mountain of french fries and generously heaped coleslaw completely covering the large oval platter set before him.

"Now I remember why I always loved eating at Harold's," Rachel said. "One meal here would be enough for the entire day."

"Are you really planning to consume all this *and* that chocolate malt?"

"It's either eat it or smuggle it out in my purse. Harold would never forgive me if I left anything on my plate." She reached for a bottle of ketchup.

"Okay, I'm game if you are." Matthew assembled his burger and took a large bite. It was delicious. His low groan of contentment earned him a small smile from Rachel; he recognized it as the first totally spontaneous smile she'd given him.

How long had it been since he'd had a meal like this? he wondered. Probably not since *he* had been in college. The restaurants he now frequented served far more sophisticated cuisine in much less quantity at ten times the price. "While we're attempting to eat all this," he said, "I'd like to hear the rest of your story." And that was the unvarnished truth. He *was* interested.

"All right," Rachel agreed, still surprised at how easy it had been to discuss her past with this man. She continued her tale, more at ease than she'd been at any time that day. "Although I came up with the concept for the store, Ava made it a reality when she suggested we make it a joint project. She recommended we use Luther's studio, which at that time took up nearly the entire ground floor of the house. It turned out to be a great idea—and a good location. Benjamin Bradford lent his advice on the legal aspects of launching a business. Ava and I each contributed an equal amount of money to redecorate and stock our initial inventory. And the business just took off.

"We made a profit—a few dollars, but a profit—at the end of the second month, and promptly spent it on a bottle of cheap champagne. The store's been profitable ever since the day we popped the cork and made a toast." She knew there was pride intertwined with the humor in her voice, and she *was* proud of what she and Ava had achieved. "Our merchandise has expanded over the last two years. Initially we sold mainly greeting cards, books and wrapping paper. Now we have an array of items."

"Including a gazebo," Matthew added. "Whose idea was that?"

"Mine. We found an old one in a backyard in Cottonwood, and I think Jack cursed under his breath the whole time he dismantled it and put in back together inside the store. I can recall a grumbled phrase that sounded suspiciously like—" she lowered her voice deeply "—'just another damn-fool notion.'"

Although the man across the table made no comment, she was certain he agreed wholeheartedly with Jackson McCarthy's assessment—even though Matthew Kent and his uncle appeared to be total opposites, at least outwardly. Yet hidden beneath Jack's somewhat ragtag appearance lurked a warm heart, Rachel thought as she took a sip of her sinfully rich malt. She wasn't at all sure what his nephew was like under his polished, professional exterior. Of course there was the remarkable temper she'd witnessed that morning. And she remembered Jack could also display quite a temper. Maybe the two men weren't really so different.

Rachel set her glass down. "Anyway, after the gazebo was in place, we decided to put in a speaker system to pipe in music."

"Violins," Matthew said around another bite of burger. His frown came and went so quickly she almost missed it.

"Among other things," she added defensively. He was no doubt as disdainful of mood music as he was of indoor gazebos. The man didn't have a romantic bone in his body. But it was a very attractive body nonetheless, she had to admit.

"Any new ideas on the horizon?" that attractive male asked after several minutes of silence.

She looked up from her plate. "New ideas?"

"Regarding merchandise for the store."

"Well, I'm thinking about stocking some games."

He cocked an eyebrow. "What kind of games?"

"There are a few 'romantic encounter' types on the mar-

ket specifically designed for two people in an intimate relationship. I've ordered a sample of one version to see
what's involved."

"Not quite like Scrabble or Monopoly, I would guess."

"I'm sure that's right," she agreed in a solemn voice
tinged with irony. "You're probably terrific at Monopoly.
All that high finance."

"I think I won my first game when I was five," he admitted.

Rachel's laugh was rueful. "I don't remember ever winning. The mysteries of Boardwalk and Park Place always
eluded me." She finished a last french fry. "I'm sure my
father despaired of me more than once, though he never
said so."

"I take it he's good with money. What does he do for a
living?"

"He was a banker."

That eyebrow went up again. "Was?"

"He's retired," Rachel said shortly, sorry she'd brought
up her father. She didn't really want to discuss him. She
was still coming to terms with her changing relationship
with her parent. "Are you done?"

If the man across from her had noted her evasiveness,
he gave no indication. He merely glanced down. "I *am*
done, though I have no idea how I ate all that."

"It's rumored Harold's food is addictive," she confided
as she sat back. "Once you start, you can't stop."

"I'll have to return and test that theory." He pushed his
plate aside and rested his forearms on the table. "After all,
I'll be here for six weeks."

She studied him. "So you're actually going to do it."

His gaze met hers head-on. "When I make a commitment, that's it," he said bluntly. "And I always finish what
I start."

Was that a promise or a warning? she wondered.

THE LEXUS PURRED like a sleek black cat as they drove back toward the lawyer's office. Matthew handled it with the respect he felt it deserved, even though it was a rental car. An intricate piece of machinery was like a woman—with just the right touch, both could provide a great deal of pleasure.

As if she'd read his thoughts, at least about the car, Rachel said, "I'll bet you drive something like this back in Denver, don't you?"

Smiling faintly, he kept his gaze on the road. Even in the middle of a lazy summer afternoon, there was some traffic and several bicycles. "Nothing quite this elaborate."

"A Lincoln? A Cadillac?"

"An eight-year-old Buick." He slanted a swift glance her way in time to see her opened mouth snap shut. "Disappointed?"

"Puzzled," she admitted. "I'm sure money isn't a problem. Why such an old car?"

"It still gives good service. And I don't like waste."

"The suit you're wearing is probably worth more than that car," she pointed out.

"But I need the suit. I don't need a new car," he said reasonably as he pulled into a small lot. There were only a few cars parked there. "Which one's yours?"

Rachel waved a hand toward the side. "Right here's fine."

Matthew stopped the Lexus behind a light brown, far-from-new Chevy sedan. He shifted in his seat to look at the woman next to him. "Now, that's a sensible automobile. Not flashy, but it has staying power. You'll get at least five more years out of it, if you take good care of it."

For a moment he thought she was going to laugh as a spark of humor flared in her eyes. Then it vanished. "I'm glad to hear that," she said seriously. "It's so important to have a car you can depend on." She paused. "Thank you for lunch."

"It was my pleasure—" he rubbed his flat stomach "—even if I did gain five pounds in the process...Rosie." He couldn't resist that last word.

She shot him a did-I-hear-right? stare. "Rosie?"

He nodded. "In honor of those invisible rose-colored glasses you view the world through."

Her eyes narrowed at that. All at once she looked as if it would please her enormously to punch him in the gut. Instead, she reached for the door handle.

"Wait, I'll come around and get it." He caught the flicker of surprise on her face. When they'd arrived at the restaurant for lunch, she'd been out of the car before he was. Obviously she wasn't accustomed to that kind of small courtesy from a man.

With that observation, he got out and walked around to open the passenger door. He extended a hand to help her out and found he didn't want to let hers go when she stood next to him. That soft, cool hand felt good in his. Too good. Once again he had the urge to kiss her...and more. Ruthlessly he wrenched his thoughts from the *more*. And then her hand trembled, just a little. Just enough to tell him she wasn't unaffected by his touch. He released her and took a step back. "I'll see you next Monday. Sometime in the afternoon, probably."

"All right," she said. Only those two carefully neutral words. Then she walked away.

He closed the car door and returned to the driver's side, wondering how she really felt about his impending visit. As he got behind the wheel, an engine started with a mighty roar. Startled, he looked up sharply and saw an older model, red Nissan 280ZX back out beside the brown sedan. It was a small sports car with a lot of power. And Rachel McCarthy was the driver.

For an instant, her provocative green eyes were reflected in his rear-view mirror. Then the Zee shot forward, turned on a dime and whipped out of the parking lot. In a flash, she was gone.

Matthew found himself shaking his head. So much for assumptions, he thought. It appeared he was in for even more surprises than he'd had in the past two days.

RACHEL DROVE down familiar streets. She gave in to the urge to laugh she'd suppressed minutes before. Clearly she had confounded the man with the steel-gray eyes. That pleased her enormously, probably because she felt so off balance whenever she was around him. It was gratifying to have the shaky shoe on the other foot for a change, if only for a moment. He was far too self-assured to be disconcerted for long.

Rachel turned onto a side street near Northern Arizona University. She hadn't been in this area since she'd moved to Jerome two years earlier. Other than some mementos she would never part with, she'd sold or given away everything before leaving, wanting to make a new start. She was on her own. Her husband was gone, and she had no children. She had wanted a child, but Danny had said he wasn't ready to be a father. So they had waited. Would he ever have been truly ready? she wondered. In some ways, her husband had never completely grown up.

"Daredevil Danny" she'd nicknamed him when they'd met in third grade. He had been a boy—and a man—who had loved to take risks. First playmates, then sweethearts, then lovers, then man and wife, they had been each other's best friend. And then Danny had taken one risk too many and tried to fly through a dangerous storm.

It was time to go home, Rachel decided, and a tap on the accelerator sent the car zooming forward in a way that lightened her spirits. She felt a little wild and crazy whenever she drove the Zee. Maybe some of that McCarthy taste for adventure had rubbed off on the prudent Rachel Wilson, she mused. Perhaps that was why she'd bought the car secondhand a year ago. It had surprised some people at the time. And Matthew Kent today.

Rachel frowned as her thoughts turned to the other episode in that parking lot. It had been the second time she'd touched him. And the second time she'd felt a jolt of heightened awareness. If she reacted that way every time she got close to him, it would be a very long six weeks.

She sighed. Something told her it was *exactly* how she was going to react, whether she wanted to or not.

3

"I STILL CAN'T believe it. You, Mr. Never-Take-A-Break, are going to be gone for *six weeks?*"

Louise Arlington could, and quite frequently did, get away with addressing her boss in such a cavalier manner. She had been with Kent Enterprises for many years, first as Andrew Kent's long-suffering secretary, then as a far-more-content assistant to his son. Not that they always agreed, Matthew reflected as he signed one last letter. His dedication to work, or "obsession," as Louise had termed it on more than one occasion, continued to be a point of contention between them.

"It's either that, Lou, or let my aunt's estate go, literally, to the dogs," he said dryly, rearranging the stack of documents he'd signed into neat, precisely placed groups. "Or, rather, to *a* dog."

Lou leaned forward and braced her delicate, pink-silk-clad arms on the sides of the ivory leather chair set beside Matthew's enormous desk. The antique pine desk had belonged to his father, as had the large office in which they now sat. That office was on the top floor of one of the tallest skyscrapers in Denver. Andrew Kent had never done anything in a small way.

"The whole thing doesn't make sense," Lou said quietly. She was a thin, silver-haired woman who smelled like orange blossoms, talked softly and carried a big, very effective stick in the form of an iron will. "I met Ava at your parents' wedding, and while I have to admit she had a flamboyant personality and clearly didn't care if people approved of her or not, she struck me as a sensible person under all that flash. It makes me suspect there's something behind these odd conditions in the will."

Matthew was fond of Lou Arlington; he also had a healthy respect for her judgment. And her words echoed the impression he still had that he'd been manipulated for some purpose. It hadn't pleased him then; it didn't please him now. He frowned. "I've got more than a hunch you're right. Yet the terms of that will remain—comply, take it to court, or put a mongrel named Hodgepodge in the upper-income bracket."

"And since you've decided against litigation, you're going back to somewhere in Arizona called Jerome," Lou calmly finished for him. "Where is this place, anyway?"

"It's about an hour's drive south of Flagstaff—an old mining city built right into the side of a mountain. Now they've turned it into a tourist area, with all sorts of small stores occupying buildings the miners abandoned when the ore ran out."

"Sounds quaint. What kind of store did your aunt own?"

Matthew had been expecting that question. Still, he braced himself as he said, "It's called the Realm of Romance—featuring a variety of useless, but apparently profitable, items like *those* novels I catch you reading every now and then."

Lou's blue eyes widened perceptibly. "*You're* going to inherit a business pushing *romance?*" She laughed...and laughed. "That's like Ebenezer Scrooge selling Christmas trees!"

Matthew ignored her amusement. "It's only a half interest in the store," he told her blandly. He went on to give a thumbnail sketch of the situation, including a deliberately offhand description of Rachel McCarthy's role.

"This gets more intriguing by the minute," Lou said

when he finished. A speculative gleam had entered her shrewd blue eyes, but she didn't pursue the subject. Instead, she asked who would handle the various facets of the business in his absence.

Not that they didn't both know, Matthew thought as they went down the list, that if a critical decision had to be made, it would be made by the deceptively fragile woman seated beside him. Everyone employed by Kent Enterprises was well aware of it. The fact that he trusted her integrity and intelligence implicitly made it easier for him to consider the time he would be out of contact. Lou Arlington ran a tight ship; the business would survive without him.

The real question was: how would *he* survive without the business?

"I STILL CAN'T believe Ava's nephew, the financial guru, would actually agree to spend six weeks here," Bonnie Gallico said as she stood beside Rachel at the bookcases. They were in the process of restocking the shelves with a new shipment of paperbacks.

Bonnie had worked for the Realm of Romance on a part-time basis since shortly after the business had opened. When Ava's health had begun to fail, Bonnie had jumped in to fill the void. As an enthusiastic supporter of the store's underlying concept, Bonnie was a tremendous asset to the operation. She was also the closest friend Rachel had in Jerome.

"He made it crystal clear he's going to do it," Rachel said, "and I don't think he's a man who would change his mind without a very good reason. Like maybe World War III."

Bonnie shifted a stack of books held in her long arms. She turned to Rachel, looking down slightly since she was two inches taller. "So the man's tenacious. And I already know he's comfortable in the cash department and not married. What else?''

Rachel straightened her T-shirt. "He's the quintessential businessman, with a truckload of confidence and a mind that zips through numbers like a high-speed calculator. He was probably born decked out in a three-piece suit, and then proceeded to count all his tiny fingers and toes in the delivery room to make sure Mother Nature hadn't shortchanged him.''

Bonnie grinned. "Sounds interesting in a *Wall-Street-Journal* kind of way. How does he look?''

Much, much too good for my peace of mind. Rachel nudged that thought aside and attempted a neutral description. "He's in his mid-thirties, tall and rather lean, with black hair cut conservatively short. Some women might find him attractive,'' she added with all the nonchalance she could summon.

"But you don't?''

Trust Bonnie to ask the relevant question, Rachel thought ruefully. With her raven hair and the large, gold-hoop earrings she usually wore, Bonnie looked like a contemporary Gypsy, and, besides having occasional "fey'' feelings regarding future events, sometimes she could be too perceptive for comfort. Like now.

"I might,'' Rachel conceded, "if I didn't suspect there are solid metal bands wrapped around his emotions.'' Which was only partly true, she admitted to herself. Emotions aside, Matthew Kent still had the physical presence to turn a woman's head—even a woman who valued emotional involvement so highly that she'd founded a business based on it.

"Well, he sounds plenty attractive to me,'' Bonnie said as she turned back to the shelves. "Too bad I'm not available.''

Rachel smiled. "I think Neil Gallico's a knockout, and

a wonderful husband and father to boot.'' And that was totally true. Bonnie's husband, a forest ranger at nearby Red Rock State Park, was the type of man Rachel had always admired. His world revolved around Bonnie and their six-year-old daughter Darcy. *All women should be as lucky as Bonnie!* Rachel reflected.

As though she'd sensed that reflection, Bonnie said, ''I *am* lucky. Neil's a great guy. Men who live life in the fast corporate lane aren't everything.''

''Or sometimes even *anything* that matters,'' Rachel felt compelled to tack on, although one man who lived in that lane was already wreaking havoc with her thoughts.

''Nevertheless, Matthew Kent will be here on Monday,'' Bonnie pointed out. ''What are you going to do with him?''

As little as possible. That silent statement summed up the situation, but Rachel wanted to give a less revealing response. ''I'm not sure,'' was all she could manage at that moment.

''We could always dress him up—or perhaps 'down' would be the appropriate word—as Eros, the god of love, and stick him in the display window,'' Bonnie suggested. ''Bound to boost sales.''

Rachel hoisted another stack of books from the carton on the floor. She refused to speculate on visions that might be conjured up if she allowed her imagination full rein. The man in question was devastating enough with all his clothes *on*.

She shook her head. ''That wouldn't work. He'd be counting customers as they came in and estimating profits at the same time—with a query on their net worth to verify his analysis. I'll have to come up with an alternate plan. Maybe just take it day by day.''

''Six weeks is a lot of days.''

''I'll think of something,'' Rachel said confidently. It was a confidence she was far from feeling. But somehow, some way she would find *something* to keep Matthew Kent occupied as the days went by, she vowed.

The real question was: how would she, herself, sleep at night with the disturbing man in the apartment below her?

HE ARRIVED on her doorstep late Monday afternoon. Since the store was closed, Rachel was finishing her weekly cleanup of the front display area when a dark blue Buick sedan pulled up to the curb. It was an older car, yet it had clearly been pampered. Sporting what looked like new tires, its paint finish shone and its chrome trim gleamed, despite a thin layer of travel dust.

Matthew Kent got out and walked around to open the trunk. Though today he was minus a suit jacket and tie, he wore sharply creased pants and a fine white cotton dress shirt. That was a long way from casual attire—at least by the standards of Jerome—even with the sleeves of that shirt rolled up to the elbows, revealing the dark hair on his forearms.

Rachel watched as those arms effortlessly lifted out two large pieces of luggage. The man might spend most of his time behind a desk, she reflected, but he appeared to be in good shape. Too good. It would suit her better if he'd had to struggle, just a little. There was something disconcerting about the thought that his body might be as powerful as his intellect.

Carrying his suitcases, Matthew started for the store. He hesitated for a split second, meeting Rachel's gaze through the window and giving her a quick nod before he continued forward.

A few steps took her to the door. She opened it and stood aside to let him enter. "Welcome back to Jerome," she found herself saying. Up to that moment, she'd had no idea how to greet him, but that friendly yet offhand comment sounded right to her. After all, though the man didn't want to be here, he *was* here, and they would have to make the best of the situation.

As if he'd come to the same conclusion, he gave her a faint smile. "It feels good to be out of that car. Where should I put these?" He still held his luggage.

"Might as well take them up to the second floor now," she told him. "The stairs are at the rear of the house. This way."

She walked through the store and down a short corridor. "The office and storeroom are back here," she said, pointing to small rooms on each side. At the end of the hall, she pushed open a sturdy outside door and held it as Matthew walked through.

He stopped dead in his tracks and stared straight ahead. *"Good God."*

Rachel had to smile at his startled expression. While it was evident when one faced the building that the house was set right on the side of the mountain, that fact couldn't be fully appreciated until it was viewed from the rear. Only a few yards of porch floor and a wooden railing stood between them and a two-thousand-foot drop. The sun, now low in the sky behind them, cast a scarlet light over the sheer cliffs visible on the far side of the vibrant green vista directly below. "That's the Verde Valley," she explained. "Quite a sight, isn't it?"

"It's spectacular. But I can't help wondering if anyone has ever fallen off this mountain."

"Not recently. Of course, after a hard day's dig for copper and a night's carousing in the saloons, I'd be willing to bet at least one miner took a tumble."

"And wound up at the pearly gates, no doubt."

"Or the more depressing alternative," she tossed in, "depending on how big a sinner that particular miner was." She closed the door. "But wherever he wound up, we'd better get moving. That luggage must be heavy."

"Not really," he said easily, confirming her thoughts about those strong arms. She started up the stairs.

Matthew watched the sway of feminine hips, once again outlined in well-fitting denim, as he followed her. In the back of his mind, he could almost see the resolutions he'd made during the drive from Denver spiraling down the proverbial drain.

He would not get involved with Rachel McCarthy.

He would treat her as a business associate, nothing more.

He would put a lid on his hormones and keep it there.

Perhaps he could still revive those intentions. Perhaps not. Just a few minutes in her company had placed the outcome in doubt. And it wasn't only those exotic eyes, he realized. Or merely her body—although what he'd been able to see of it was pleasing. It was all of that, plus her quick mind and her sense of humor...and something else. Some attribute that seemed to be hers alone—that he hadn't been able to figure out. Whatever it was, it held a powerful attraction for him. *Dammit.*

When they reached the back door on the second floor, Rachel slid a key in the lock and a dog began to bark. It swiftly became a crescendo of sound as she opened the door. "It's me, sweetie," she said, walking in. Immediately the barking stopped.

Matthew entered a step behind her and deposited his luggage against a nearby wall while Rachel shut the door and continued to murmur soft reassurances. He straightened and turned to find himself being studied by an animal the likes of which he'd never seen before. It had the rugged build and dense dark hair of a German shepherd, the long legs and narrow-muzzled face of a collie, and the drooping ears of a beagle. The dog was probably middle-aged in canine years, yet Matthew noted a youthful spark in the black eyes that assessed him.

"Now there's a clear case of canine genes run amuck,"

he stated dryly. "It's Lassie meets Snoopy by way of Rin Tin Tin. In fact, it appears to be a combination of almost every breed known to man."

Rachel laughed softly. "That's pretty much what Ava thought—which is why she named him Hodgepodge."

At the sound of his name, Hodgepodge began to thump a long tail against the colorful braided rug that covered the tiled floor of the small entryway. Just steps away was a large kitchen bordered by oak cabinets and yellow countertops. Matthew had barely taken in those details when the dog left Rachel's side to move toward him hesitantly.

Matthew hunkered down and held out a hand. "So you're the mongrel with delusions of grandeur. Well, I'm not about to let you get your grubby paws on my aunt's estate."

Hodgepodge took a cautious whiff of his long fingers. Then, in an instant, he let out a joyful yelp and launched forward. Taken completely by surprise, Matthew found himself sprawled on the floor with his back against the wall and two large paws on his shoulders. A moist tongue got one lick at his face before he grasped a leather collar to pull the dog's head away from him.

"Sit down," he ordered, quietly but with implacable authority. Hodgepodge immediately obeyed and sat back on his haunches, his tongue draped over one side of his mouth as he panted enthusiastically, tail wagging a mile a minute.

"I've never seen him react like that to anyone," Rachel said with astonishment.

Matthew got to his feet and brushed his palms on his pants. "You won't see him acting like that again. Not with me. He needs a firm hand."

"No, really, Matthew. I mean it. He's *never* acted that way—even with Ava, who he seemed to regard as his savior, and with good reason. He was lying on the side of the road, injured by some type of accident, when she picked

him up and took him to a vet. Still, he didn't display that
degree of affection with her—or anyone, until now. You
must be very good with dogs.''

Matthew shoved his hands in his pockets and studied the
animal seated before him. "You're wrong. I've never
owned a dog. Hell, I don't even particularly *like* dogs.''
After those blunt words, he slanted a glance at Rachel, who
stood with arms folded beneath her breasts and a bemused
smile on her face.

"Well, this one definitely likes you," she told him.

Once again he gazed at the subject under discussion. The
black eyes that looked back at him shone with something
undeniably close to adoration. *That's just great, Kent,* he
groused to himself. *As if things weren't complicated
enough, now you've got a lovesick mongrel to deal with.*

RACHEL GAVE MATTHEW a tour of the apartment, feeling
that good manners demanded it. She glanced over her
shoulder as they began, and swallowed a chuckle when she
saw Hodgepodge following behind, nose held inches away
from the pant legs of a man who totally ignored that de-
votion. They walked down a long hallway, past the kitchen
and small adjoining dining area, to a large living room with
three tall, narrow windows set into the front wall of the
building.

Ava LaMont had decorated this room, and much of the
rest of the apartment, with lace curtains, bright chintz fabrics and soft, plump furniture built for comfort, not mere
display. Rachel admired it so much that she'd used some
of the same ideas in furnishing hers. Yet the one outstand-
ing feature of this room could be found nowhere else in
the world. It was a huge oil painting practically covering
one long wall. Vividly it portrayed the sun's brilliant rays
piercing through dark clouds to light the legendary red-
tinged rocks of nearby Sedona.

"It's a Luther LaMont," she explained, pointing to the black slashes resembling two *L*s in a bottom corner. "This is the painting Ava left me. I haven't been able to move it upstairs yet. There's one more painting out at the cabin. Everything else was either sold before Luther died or destroyed in the crash."

"Quite impressive," Matthew commented, and then walked over to one of the windows with the dog trailing him. He brushed aside a lacy white panel and looked out. "What's all the activity across the street?"

Rachel moved to stand beside him. She knew he referred to several construction vehicles parked on the side of a large, four-story brick building that had lost its doors and windows. Two laborers tossed debris from a window opening to a dump truck below. "Back at the turn of the century, that place was an apartment house for miners. Somewhere along the way, the top floors were closed off, and the ground floor was last used by a local sculptor. Now, new owners are completely renovating the inside to convert it into a small hotel."

Abruptly he let the curtain drop and turned to face her. In a heartbeat, she became aware of how close she was to him. Close enough to smell the slightly musky, all-male scent of him. Close enough to hear him breathing. Close enough to jump-start her own breath. Far too close for comfort.

Taking a step back, she cleared her throat. "There are three bedrooms in the apartment," she forced out. The very last thing she wanted to talk about was *bedrooms*, but she knew it had to be done before she could leave. "The largest, which was Ava's, is off this room—" she waved a hand in the direction of a door on the left "—and next to it is a smaller one Jack's been using when he's in town. The third bedroom is at the rear of the house, across from the kitchen."

"I'll take the back one. The view has to be great."

It wasn't what she wanted to hear. Since the second and third floor apartments were identical in configuration and she slept in the upstairs back bedroom, it meant he'd be sleeping exactly one floor below her. But she could hardly argue with him about it. She nodded. "All right, then, I'll leave you to get settled. Since it's pretty late in the day, perhaps I could show you the office and the rest of the operation tomorrow?"

"That's fine." He hesitated as if debating something, then added, "Will you have dinner with me tonight?"

She should have expected the invitation. After all, she thought, he didn't know anyone else here, and he probably didn't want to eat alone. But *she* didn't want to set a precedent. Living in the same house, it would be all too easy to fall into the habit of spending time with him outside of business. Still, since it was his first day here, she might have accepted—if she hadn't been so thoroughly rattled by his closeness a moment earlier. "I'm sorry, I can't. I have…things to do."

Gray eyes studied her thoughtfully as he said, "That's all right. Perhaps another time."

Now she felt guilty. Which was absolutely ridiculous, she told herself. It didn't help. "If you'd rather not go out," she said, attempting to ease her conscience, "I stocked the refrigerator and freezer on Saturday. And all the basics are in the kitchen cabinets. You won't have to shop for a while."

His smile was faint. "I'm not much of a cook, but I'll manage. I'm not much of a shopper, either. Thank you for thinking of that. You'll have to let me reimburse you."

Rachel shook her head. "Ava did the same thing for me when I moved here." She smiled briefly at the memory. "She wouldn't take any money, and I can be just as stubborn. Besides, Jerome's a small enough place that most people seem to look out for each other. It's one of the best things about living here.''

"Okay, I'll accept that," Matthew said, "but now I am definitely treating you to a meal sometime.'' She opened her mouth to protest. "*Not* to pay you back," he continued. "Just as a friendly gesture to a fellow resident of Jerome.''

"We'll see," was the only comment she could come up with as she turned and started for the back door.

"Aren't you forgetting something?''

That question brought her up short. She glanced over her shoulder to see him standing in the same spot, one eyebrow raised quizzically. Then he looked down at the dog stretched out on the carpet, furry head resting on a highly polished shoe with every appearance of bliss.

Sighing at the fact that her thought processes seemed to have abandoned her, she turned around. "You're right. It's time for his afternoon walk. Then I'll take him upstairs with me. Come on, Hodgepodge, let's go." Hodgepodge raised his head but didn't get up. Even the magic word "walk," which Rachel repeated several times over the next few minutes, had little effect. Then she tried "bone," knowing bone-shaped dog treats were a favorite. That usually drew some ardent panting from Hodgepodge, but not this time.

Just as she was about to admit defeat, Matthew said, "You might as well leave him here with me. I'll unpack and take him for a walk." When voiced by Matthew, the magic word produced immediate results. Hodgepodge jumped up expectantly.

"Not yet," Matthew muttered. Hodgepodge sat down. "Well, he may be a mongrel, but at least he appears to have a brain.''

"Are you sure you want to keep him?" Rachel felt obliged to ask, though she had no idea what she would do if he changed his mind. The dog was too big for her to carry.

His faint smile returned. "It appears I'm stuck with him for the time being. Don't worry about it. We'll work it out."

"All right. I have to admit he preferred to stay here even before he met you, maybe because he felt closer to Ava here. I've tried keeping him with me at night, but he always seemed to be restless. Anyway, I fed him his main meal earlier today, but there are some treats in the kitchen cabinet above the sink, next to a sack of dry dog food."

Matthew's smile widened just a bit. "Would those treats have anything to do with your mention of 'bones'?"

Hodgepodge gave an ecstatic bark.

SEVERAL HOURS LATER Hodgepodge had been walked and given a few of the treasured "bones," and Matthew had fixed himself a ham sandwich with a glass of milk for dinner.

Now he sat on the sofa in the living room, studying the vibrant painting on the wall across from him. Luther LaMont had clearly possessed talent. In New York, or any large, cosmopolitan city, that talent would no doubt have created quite a stir. Yet LaMont had chosen to live off the beaten path in Jerome. What had the talented man been like? Matthew wondered. And what had he thought of the McCarthys? Probably more than Matthew's father had. Yet both had married McCarthy women.

Matthew couldn't remember much about his mother, other than that she had been physically frail. Nevertheless, photographs he'd seen had captured Rosalind McCarthy Kent's delicate beauty—a beauty that must have drawn Andrew Kent to her despite his aversion to the rest of the McCarthy siblings.

Matthew remembered even less about those McCarthys. His only memory of Ava was at some sort of party. She'd been wearing an enormous picture hat and laughing merrily. He had no idea who she had been married to, or even if she had been married, at the time. He couldn't remember Raymond—Rachel's former father-in-law—at all. His most clear recollection was of Jackson McCarthy arguing with his father. That had stuck in his mind. The two men had definitely not liked each other.

When his mother had died after a short illness, her sister and brothers had also departed from his life, never to be seen again. It wasn't until later that he realized his father had cut off the connection. After that it had been just the two of them, if you didn't count a houseful of servants, and his father had raised him to harness his emotions and deal with life on a rational basis—not like the McCarthys.

Yet, in spite of that upbringing, he had let emotion rule and married a young woman who had turned out to be totally wrong for him. Or, rather, they had been totally wrong for each other. The swift divorce that had followed had been a relief for both of them...and he had finally learned his lesson.

Matthew shifted his gaze away from the painting he'd been staring at and wiped out thoughts of the past, telling himself it was far more productive to consider the future.

And, at the moment, the future included Rachel McCarthy.

"She looked like a deer caught in the high beams when you asked her out to dinner, Kent," he mused out loud.

His faithful canine companion, reclining on the floor in front of him, issued a soft "Woof."

"So you think so too, do you, mutt?" he said with a downward glance, and received another "Woof" in response.

Matthew leaned back and lifted his arms to lace his fingers behind his head. "She means to keep her distance, that's for sure. But then, she's clearly not as fond of me as you are."

Quickly rising, Hodgepodge looked ready to lunge forward.

"Don't even think about it," Matthew warned softly. Hodgepodge stayed put. "If I wanted to be kissed, it wouldn't be by your sticky tongue, mutt. I'd be willing to wager there's someone in the house who'd do a much better job of it, if those seductive green eyes are any indication. And I'll bet her lips would be soft. Geez, I'll bet she'd be soft all over."

Visions of *all over* started to do things to his body, so he obliterated them from his mind and said, "Of course, she's not a glamorous beauty." A sharp bark followed that remark. "Well, she's not, mutt. Not that it seems to be making any difference, I have to admit. I think she could drive me crazy…if I'd let it happen. But I won't." Complete silence greeted that statement.

Matthew grimaced ruefully and got to his feet. "You probably think I have no control at all, mutt, since I've lost enough of my wits to discuss the situation with a *dog*." He switched off the lights in the living room, then started toward the rear of the house. "It's definitely time to get some sleep."

A minute later Matthew shut the back bedroom door in his faithful companion's furry face and began to remove his clothes.

Five minutes later he lay in bed, listening to soft, mournful whimpering coming from the hallway, and told himself it would stop—eventually.

Ten minutes later, wearing only his briefs, he got up and threw open the door. Hodgepodge streaked into the room and stretched out on the rug next to the bed with a contented growl.

"Don't think you can get away with this every night," Matthew grumbled as he got back under the covers. Events had somehow gotten away from him today, he reflected grimly. But tomorrow, and for the rest of the time he spent here, he'd be in firm control. It was, after all, a state that came naturally to him. He might be half McCarthy...but he was also half Kent.

Hodgepodge started to snore.

4

MATTHEW KENT COULD BRING order to an elephant stampede.

Rachel came to that conclusion one week after he'd begun his stay in Jerome. It had started to become clear when, obviously bored with his enforced vacation, he'd rearranged the contents of the store's "lotion and potion" cabinet. Jars, boxes and bottles, once haphazardly displayed, now marched together in several precisely placed rows, like a random collection of mismatched soldiers whipped into shape by a meticulous commanding officer.

And that had been only the beginning of his efforts.

The various bags of potpourri scents now reposed on the table in firm alphabetical order, from Ardently Aromatic to Viva La Violet. The greeting cards were similarly racked from Anniversary to Wedding. The candles were grouped by size and color, as were the T-shirts and everything else possessing a size and/or color—except the items in the lingerie section. The orderly man had given that particular area a wide berth.

Rachel had accepted all these painstaking rearrangements—had, in fact, encouraged them, though she'd had to grit her teeth a time or two—because she wanted to keep him as busy as she could. It had also helped to establish their relationship as business associates, and kept the emphasis off anything personal.

She wasn't ready for personal.

To that end, she'd also asked his advice about the store's

financial procedures. And there she'd struck pay dirt. It had turned into a project that could keep him occupied for some time. Where money was involved, Matthew was obviously in his element, and the amount involved didn't seem to matter. He'd begun to study the records just as closely as he would no doubt have gone through those of a multinational corporation. He'd even recommended some accounting and inventory-control programs for the store's computer, and had left late that morning for Flagstaff to look for the software he had in mind.

She, herself, had had a productive Monday, Rachel thought, inserting a manila folder into the top drawer of one of the office file cabinets. She had gotten most of her I-hate-to-do-it-but-I-absolutely-have-to filing done. If Matthew Kent could be organized, so could she.

Just then Rachel heard familiar footsteps coming down the corridor toward the office. He was back earlier than she'd expected. Apparently the man shopped as efficiently as he did everything else.

Matthew entered the room a moment later, carrying a large bag from a computer-supply store. Again he wore sharply creased pants and a crisp white shirt, sleeves rolled up to the elbows and two buttons opened at the neck to reveal dark chest hair. Rachel had come to think of it as his everyday "casual" attire. The combination laundry and cleaners she'd recommended would do a brisk business if he meant to spend six weeks dressed like this, she mused wryly. Glancing past him, she saw Hodgepodge following in his wake. It was a frequent sight these days.

She leaned back in her chair. "Looks like you two have been successful in your mission."

Matthew set the bag down on the modern oak desk and began to remove its contents. "I found everything we need. When these programs are installed and the data entered, this operation will have a much more efficient system to keep track of its records.''

Once again Rachel gritted her teeth and bit back the urge to remind him that the store had been functioning quite well before he came to Jerome. But in this case, it would be just plain petty of her, she realized. The man was light years beyond her when it came to business savvy. She shouldn't—wouldn't—resent his plan to institute this type of improvement. After all, she had encouraged him to get involved.

Yet that didn't mean she had to stay and watch the way his black hair gleamed under the overhead light. Or the way his long fingers oh-so-competently opened the boxes of software. Not to mention the way his firm mouth tightened in concentration as he leaned one narrow hip against the desk and looked over his purchases. No, she'd be far better off *not* watching him. She had more filing to do, but that could be accomplished later tonight when she could be alone.

''Well, since you know where everything is now, I'll leave you to get to it.'' She got up, gave Hodgepodge a pat on the head and started for the door. ''I've got things to do.''

Matthew lifted his gaze and observed her quick departure. *Things to do,* he thought as he sat down in the chair she'd vacated. She always had those unspecified things to do, particularly when he'd asked her out to dinner, as he had twice in the last week. Even lunch had been declined. Which had only made him more determined to press the matter, though he knew it wasn't a wise move. It would be far simpler to keep their dealings on a strictly business basis.

The bottom line, however, was that her repeated refusals had provided a challenge—one he found irresistible. Why? Perhaps it was the memory of Harold's Hamburger Heaven and the surprising woman in the red sports car he'd discovered after that lunch. She'd share another meal with him, he vowed.

MUCH LATER that evening Matthew was back at the computer, attempting to work off a pounding headache that had hit him after the uninspiring dinner he'd fixed for himself. The aspirin he'd taken two hours before hadn't brought much relief, maybe because it was his third killer headache in five days.

Grimly resolving to ignore it, he continued entering data for some time, until the dog sprawled on the white-tiled floor next to the desk woofed softly. His concentration broken, Matthew turned his head and saw the office door opening. Then Rachel appeared in the shadows by the doorway, still wearing the jeans and loose beige T-shirt she'd had on earlier. He'd come to think of that combination as her usual mode of dress. And, as usual, the shirt was one the store carried; its inscription declared Love May Be Blind, But It Can Feel Real Good. Once again her long brown hair was caught up in a ponytail.

For a second she looked unpleasantly surprised to see him, before her expression switched to the friendly yet impersonal one she invariably assumed when she dealt with him. Tonight, it irritated him more than the tenacious hammering in his brain.

"I didn't think you'd be working this late," she said quietly. She walked past the file cabinets, her steps silenced by the rubber soles of her canvas shoes, and entered the circle of illumination provided by a small brass desk lamp. "It's pretty dark in here. Don't you want the overhead light on?"

Matthew shook his head and frowned at the stab of pain that motion produced. "The brightness bothered me, so I shut it off.'' He leaned back in the brown leather swivel chair and gazed up at her. ''Why did you come down?''

''I had some filing to do, but it can wait.'' With those words, she crossed her arms and studied him for a moment. ''Headache?'' she asked sympathetically.

''How did you know?''

''The light bothering you. Plus that frown and the tense set of your shoulders. I'd bet it's not a mild one, either.''

He shrugged. ''I've had worse, I suppose.'' He lifted a hand and rubbed the bridge of his nose with his thumb and forefinger. ''Only never as many in such a short time.''

''You know, you might be going through withdrawal.''

Stunned, he dropped his hand and stared at her. *''What?''*

Her sudden smile, though faint, was clearly amused. ''You're used to a certain kind of life-style. Now, you're faced with something totally different. If you've been addicted to work, it's bound to be a big adjustment.''

''I am not *addicted* to work,'' he muttered darkly. He didn't like that word—at all.

''Oh, of course not,'' she said in exaggerated agreement. ''But, for the record, how many hours do you usually put in during a week?''

''I don't know. I never counted them.'' Which was totally true, he just realized at that moment. He'd never taken time to count them.

''Mmm-hmm. What about weekends?''

His frown deepened. ''What about them?''

''Do you work on weekends?''

''When I have to,'' he admitted. He didn't add that he'd almost always felt he had to.

Rachel nodded sagely, as if she was aware of everything he hadn't said. ''It's withdrawal.''

He wanted to argue the point, but an abrupt change in her demeanor stopped him. She seemed to be waging an internal debate as she tapped one neatly rounded, unpolished fingernail on the desk. Curious to discover the issue, he remained silent.

"I have something that might help, if you're willing to give it a try," she said at last. "It's…aromatherapy."

He killed a smirk when he saw she was completely serious. "You're going to cure my headache with *perfume?*"

This time, she was the one who frowned. "It's not perfume. It's a precise mixture of oils that can be therapeutic. We have a selection in the cabinet with the lotions. Remember those little plastic vials you lined up so neatly in the front row?"

He heard the irony in that question. Was she mocking him? No, he decided, she'd actually encouraged him to rearrange things. "I thought they were bath oil."

"Uh-uh. They're botanical oils, and there's a special blend for relieving headaches."

"Do I have to chant some mumbo jumbo and drink the stuff?"

She sighed hard enough to let him know he was trying her patience. "It's not black magic, either, Matthew. Actually, it's a combination of inhaling the scent and having the oil rubbed into the skin."

She'd be rubbing his skin? That thought seized his mind and refused to let go. He gave up the battle without much effort. "I'm willing to try it," he said with feigned offhandedness.

"Okay, I'll be right back." With that, she pivoted on her heel and turned away. "You'll have to fold the collar of your shirt under, so I can get at your neck." After tossing those last words over her shoulder, she walked out of the office.

Matthew looked at Hodgepodge. "First it's my head, then it's my neck. This experiment could prove to be extremely interesting, mutt."

In the store area seconds later, Rachel gathered the items she would need and conducted an inward dispute with a tiny voice inside her that contended she'd just made a big mistake. *But the man is clearly in pain,* her mind countered in an attempt to justify her decision. And there was nothing really personal involved in aiding a fellow human being. He was hurting; she would try to help. It was as simple as that.

Yet the persistent voice lingered as she returned to the office, whispering that where her reaction to Matthew Kent was concerned, nothing was even close to simple. *Well, it's too late now,* she silently replied and walked through the doorway.

Matthew had followed instructions and tucked in the collar of his shirt. Deciding to proceed in a no-nonsense fashion, Rachel arranged the items she'd brought with her on the desk. Then she struck a match and lit a small green candle. A delicate fragrance began to permeate the air. Out of the corner of her eye, she saw the edge of his mouth quirk upward, but he made no comment. If he was skeptical—and she'd wager her last nickel *and* the gazebo he was—he was keeping it to himself.

"The candle gives off an essence containing jasmine and lavender," she explained. "Both are used to promote relaxation." In its flickering glow, she opened two vials of oil and poured a few drops from each into the palm of her hand. "This is a combination of sweet marjoram to relieve pain, and Roman chamomile, for soothing. Tip your head forward, and we'll see if it works for you."

Matthew complied, figuring he had nothing to lose and a rubdown to gain. Rachel began to spread oil over his skin; it tingled slightly. He closed his eyes and suppressed a moan as her soft fingers gently began to knead the flesh at the base of his skull. Gradually he could feel the tight muscles unwinding, inch by inch…little by little…one by one.

Next came the area behind his ears, and he discovered that particular spot could be an erogenous zone. Strange, in all his thirty-six years and with his varied sexual experience, he hadn't known that—until Rachel touched him there and his heartbeat quickened in response. By the time she moved on minutes later, his whole body had quickened.

Yet the feel of her fingers, languidly rubbing his temples and brushing featherlight strokes across his forehead, also relaxed him. It was arousing and soothing at the same time. He'd never felt anything like it. And it went on for what seemed like forever, yet turned out to be not nearly long enough when she took her hands away.

"How do you feel?" she asked quietly, using a tissue to remove traces of oil that hadn't been absorbed.

As if I fell off the mountain and wound up in heaven. He couldn't voice that thought, though, so he said, "Better."

He couldn't see her smile, but he could feel it. "And your headache?" she asked far too politely.

He opened his eyes and shifted to look at her over his shoulder. Even before he answered, he saw her smile turn smug. "As you probably well know, it's gone." He paused. "I have to thank you. It's bizarre, but somehow it worked."

Her gaze was amused. "You're very welcome, though I can't resist the urge to mention that I told you so." Walking around, she moved next to his chair and reached for another tissue from a box on the desk. "Close your eyes and sit back for a minute while I clean up. Let your body relax completely."

Matthew obeyed. At least he shut his eyes and leaned back. His body, however, was still more than half-aroused. Forget it, he told his libido as he took a deep, steadying breath. This wasn't the right time or place...or the right woman, for that matter. But while his mind recognized those facts, his hormones were slower to concede. Waiting, he unfolded his shirt collar, then clasped his hands behind his head and determinedly contemplated the most thoroughly unarousing subject he could come up with: the Internal Revenue Service.

Rachel looked down to wipe oil off her fingers and saw them start to shake with tiny tremors. That niggling little voice had been right, she thought as she blew out the candle and put the cap back on one of the vials. She couldn't touch this man casually. Though she'd done an admirable job of concealing that fact, if she did say so herself. She'd even been able to tease him a bit.

Now, however, the physical reaction she'd kept under control had taken over, and it wouldn't be wise to prolong the situation. She needed to clear off the desk, put the items back in the store area, and return to her apartment. Fast.

Too fast for trembling fingers, it seemed, when she only succeeded in bungling her hasty attempt to cap the second vial; it leaped out of her hand and plummeted to the floor. A stream of liquid spurted onto the white tiles. And then events went swiftly out of control.

Hodgepodge jumped up and lunged toward it to investigate. Rachel took one step forward to stop the dog and felt her foot slide out from under her as it met the edge of the oil, sending her reeling backward, arms flailing uselessly. There was no time to utter a sound—no time to even think—before the back of her legs met the padded arm of the chair next to her.

In an instant, Rachel landed in the middle of Matthew's lap.

In an instant, his eyes flashed open and his arms came down.

In an instant, they were gazing at each other.

"I...spilt some oil and slipped," she murmured after a full five seconds of taut silence. *Get up!* that tiny voice inside her commanded. But she couldn't make herself move. In fact, she could barely breathe as she felt his hard thighs under her backside—and another, even more breathtaking hardness against her hip. "I'm sorry I fell on you," she managed to add.

His expression, which had conveyed merely surprise up to that moment, turned intense and purposeful. "That's okay. I don't mind at all." His low voice held more than a hint of huskiness. "Besides, I'm the one who should be sorry—and I probably will be, later—but not now." With that, his large hands grasped her upper arms and tugged her closer.

What had he meant by that last statement? The question flitted through her mind, only to be abruptly wiped out by the realization that he was about to kiss her.

"I don't think this is a good idea," she said desperately as he lowered his head. Still, she was unable to make even a token effort to pull away.

"I *know* it's not," he replied grimly before covering her mouth with his.

Nothing could have prepared Rachel for the forceful impact as their lips met, since she had never experienced anything approaching it. It was an utterly devastating sensation—like being run over by the emotional equivalent of a ten-ton truck that ruthlessly flattened resistance and generated a heady excitement as it roared through her at a breakneck speed. When Matthew slanted his mouth and stroked his tongue over her lips, she opened them for him with unquestioning acceptance.

Quite simply, she had to.

Then his strong arms encircled her, bringing her tighter to his unyielding chest, and she could feel his heart thudding against her breast. Whatever his doubts about the wisdom of the kiss, she knew he was as caught up in it as she. It was a comforting thought, until he suddenly groaned and began to thrust his tongue into her mouth repeatedly, and thought and comfort fled before the onslaught, leaving only edgy sensation and an awakening need for more.

She would give in to it…just for a moment.

Yet when he lifted his head after long moments had passed, she had to clench her jaw to restrain a protest at the desertion. With a great deal of effort, she accomplished that and opened her eyes, which had drifted closed. She looked up at him.

What she saw amazed her.

His eyes—those steel-gray eyes—were heat-tinged and smoky with desire. She would never have suspected he was capable of such depth of sensuality, but his blazing stare was searing. No other man had ever gazed at her that way. And they had only kissed! How would he look at her if they had—

Disconcerted by the wayward turn her thoughts had taken and his continued unwavering stare, she placed her palms flat against his chest, feeling the solid wall of muscle under the soft cotton of his shirt, and levered her upper body as far away as she could with his arms still holding her tightly. It wasn't far.

"Not yet," he told her, very softly, very firmly. Then he started to run his long fingers over her back in a gentle motion, as if to soothe her into submission. "I have to taste you again. If I were fool enough to believe in such things, I'd say you were a green-eyed witch who's cast a spell on me." Inexorably he pulled her toward him. "Do you want to taste me again, Rachel?"

Without even thinking, she nodded—only once.

He took a harsh, ragged breath. "Then put your arms around me…and let's taste each other."

Obediently she lifted her arms and wrapped them around his neck, as though he were the one who had cast the spell.

Matthew began the kiss more slowly than the one before. Rachel had accepted him then, but now he wanted her active participation. To that end, he curbed the impulse to plunder and sent his lips on a leisurely exploration of her mouth, moving at a languid pace from one corner to the other, then back to the silky center. Her lower lip was fuller now from the effects of the earlier kiss. Abruptly he caught the swollen lip between his teeth, sucked it into his mouth and held her captive for several long seconds, until he felt a shiver flow through the soft body pressed against him from hip to breast to shoulder.

It was the reaction he'd been waiting for.

Now his teeth released her, but only to let him cover her mouth with his own. Delving into warmth and moistness, he felt her small tongue hesitantly tangle with his. He knew she was unsure; he'd been prepared for that. What intrigued him was the subtle yet unmistakable suggestion of freshness in her response. Although she had been married, Rachel McCarthy was not a truly experienced lover. He was certain of that. Nevertheless, she *was* responding. Beautifully. His own reaction took a swift dive from his brain to his groin, immeasurably strengthening the urge to plunder...so he did.

Matthew deepened the kiss and quickly lost a part of himself in the honeyed taste and satiny textures of the woman in his arms. Minutes later, however, when he had to fist his hands to prevent his fingers from roaming all— *all*—over her body, the other portion of him always in control told him to either end it or be prepared to take it to the limit. Her effect on him was becoming too potent for compromise. So he had to end it. He was about to do exactly that when Hodgepodge gave a low bark.

While Rachel kept right on kissing him, clearly hearing nothing, Matthew stilled completely. He knew that sound, having heard it several times in relation to himself. The bark had been a welcome rather than a warning. The dog had just become aware of something or someone and was happy about it. Matthew wanted to believe it was a some-*thing*, but instincts sharpened by travel in some risky places veered to the side of some*one*.

Slowly, trying not to startle her, he grasped Rachel's arms and broke their stranglehold on his neck. Then he lifted his mouth from hers and gazed down at her long-lashed eyes as they opened listlessly. He nearly groaned when he saw how clouded and dazed they were. He was responsible for that look; he had to protect her from outward intrusion until she could get her bearings and return to reality. Gently he tucked her head under his chin and pressed it against one broad shoulder. Then, holding her close, he swiveled the chair around to face the doorway.

There was indeed someone leaning against the door frame, watching them intently.

"THAT'S QUITE a story," Jackson McCarthy said as he poured himself a second shot of twelve-year-old bourbon. "I'm almost sorry I missed that meeting with the stuffed-shirt lawyer, even if his legalese is more than I can stomach. But I have to admit Ben Bradford's a shrewd bird, Matt."

Irritated by the shortening of his name, though deciding not to make an issue of it, Matthew faced his uncle across the round dining-room table. He could hardly object to "Matt" when the older man had already insisted on being called merely "Jack."

"I got the same impression about Bradford," Matthew said, frowning. "In fact, I think he's up to something. What, I haven't been able to figure out."

"Hmm. You could damn well be right." With that, Jack reclined in the ladder-back oak dining chair, angled his long, khaki-covered legs out in front of him, and took a short swallow of his drink. His shaggy dark hair was long enough to cover the collar of his khaki shirt. His deeply tanned forehead, one of the few portions of facial skin not concealed by a dark beard, furrowed in contemplation.

Matthew assumed it was his own unexpected presence in Jerome, together with the surprising developments he'd just related concerning the will, that had so far deflected any remark from his uncle regarding the scene in the office less than an hour before. There would be some comment eventually, he was certain; he was prepared to deal with it.

Sipping his bourbon, Matthew thought about Rachel's reaction after he'd whispered the unwelcome news that they had a visitor. In thirty seconds flat, she'd managed to scramble off his lap, make a babbling, barely coherent introduction, take a few ineffective swipes at the oil on the floor, give Jackson McCarthy a hasty hug, and whisk herself out the door with the familiar excuse of "things" to be done.

And Matthew had been left facing the all-too-knowing gaze of a tall, rangy male in his mid-fifties whose appearance was probably best described as a combination of mountain man and desert rat—both in conspicuous need of a shower.

Now that shower had been taken, Matthew's newly purchased, aged liquor had been offered and appreciatively accepted, and uncle and nephew were getting to know each other. Or, rather, they were circling like two wary males of most any species, each somewhat unsure of the other.

"Do you remember me?" Jack asked, splitting the silence.

"Vaguely," Matthew replied. "I can recall a time when you were arguing with my father."

Jack's laugh was brief and humorless. "I was always arguing with your father. That only ceased when your mother died and the McCarthys were declared a lot less than welcome in the Kent household." He lifted his glass and took another swallow. "I still remember the huge Kent home, though. It was quite a showplace. Do you still live there?''

''No, I sold it after my father died.'' He didn't add that he hadn't lived there since he'd left for college. ''I have a condo in downtown Denver.''

''So you can scurry back and forth to the office without wasting a minute?''

Disregarding the sarcasm in that question, Matthew merely replied, ''It's convenient.'' Then he propped his elbows on the table and leaned forward. It was time to take the conversation into the other man's territory. ''What do *you* do for a living?''

Jack grinned a wily grin. ''From the look of me now, you probably think not much—and you'd be partly right. I only work four months out of the year. The rest of the time, I do exactly what I want to do—lay out under the stars on warm nights, build a fire in my cabin on cold ones, fish the rivers around here for my dinner, and mind my own business…most of the time.''

''Admirable,'' Matthew said dryly. ''What about those four months as a member of the working class?''

Rather than being offended at the implied criticism, Jack's brown eyes were amused. ''Oh, I don't know if I'd go so far as to actually call it 'working.' It's more like slinging hash on a grandiose scale. I'm a chef.''

''A *chef*.'' Matthew prided himself on his ability to judge a person, but he knew he'd been way off base in this case. The man who dressed like Indiana Jones obviously had another side to him.

''One of the ritziest resorts in the Phoenix area pays me a good deal of money to satisfy the discriminating palates of Arizona's wealthy winter visitors. Some of them even appreciate my efforts. Then spring rolls around, and I can leave again with more than enough cash to keep me going until the next year.''

"Don't you ever get bored?"

"Never." The word was stated with clear, straightforward honesty. "There's no reason to be bored or restless when you're content with your life. I am with mine." Suddenly Jackson's brown eyes turned intent. "How are you coping with your 'vacation'?"

Although he understood there was more to that question than simple curiosity, Matthew only shrugged. "It hasn't been easy."

"Strange...it looked like you were enjoying yourself when I first laid eyes on you tonight."

Here it comes, Kent. He met his uncle's knowing gaze head-on. "Not that I think it's any of your business, but, just for the record, Rachel and I are not involved with each other." His low voice was edged with steel. "Tonight was an accident."

Several seconds of silence passed before Jack said wisely, "Fate has a way of arranging accidents, Matt."

Matthew grimaced. "A philosopher as well as a chef?"

Jack's wily grin returned. "On occasion." Then that grin vanished. "But you're right, it's none of my business. It's just that I'm fond of Rachel. She was devastated when Danny died. I'd hate to see her hurt again. She'd be a mighty good woman...for the right man."

"And you don't think I'm the right man."

"More to the point, do you?" Jack countered as he sat forward and put down his empty glass.

"No." Matthew's grudging reply was forced by his sense of honesty. "Not that it makes much difference," he added, shrugging. "Contrary to what you saw tonight, Rachel does her best to avoid me outside of business hours."

"Hmm." Jack's expression turned thoughtful as he rose to his bare feet. "Somehow that doesn't surprise me. You probably remind her of her father."

Matthew was rendered speechless as Jack muttered a

good-night and left him sitting at the table, staring straight ahead.

He reminded Rachel of her father? *Why?* It couldn't be because of his age. He was, after all, only seven years older than Rachel—although he was much older in other ways, he had to admit. It was the reason for his negative reply to Jack's last, far-too-perceptive question.

Logically, Matthew knew he wasn't the "right" man for Rachel. She was a romantic; he was a realist. She still had her ideals; his were long gone. Their differences went on and on. Once he had ignored differences and the result had been disastrous.

And, added to all of that, tonight he'd tasted the intriguing freshness of Rachel's kiss. Even sexually, he was far more experienced than she. Perversely, that fact—and knowing she could respond to him so beautifully—only strengthened his physical desire for her.

Dammit! He couldn't remind her of her father! Yet those had been Jackson McCarthy's very words, and he'd been completely serious when he'd uttered them.

What the devil did he mean?

5

"SO I'VE DECIDED to shave my head, put a ring through my nose and join a commune in the Yukon," Bonnie was saying in a steadily rising tone.

Rachel blinked. "Huh?" She was seated on a tall stool behind the store's front counter. It was Saturday, lunchtime was approaching, and there was a lull in the steady stream of customers who had been coming in since the store had opened at nine o'clock. Her thoughts had drifted—as they'd already done a hundred times—back to Monday night's events.

Bonnie's hoop earrings swung gently as she walked forward. Today she wore a yellow cotton sundress. "Wonderful to have you back, Rachel, for however long it lasts. This is the third day I've been talking mostly to myself."

Bonnie regularly worked Thursday through Sunday. Since her widowed grandmother lived with her, there was usually someone home to take care of Darcy outside of school hours. When there wasn't, Bonnie brought her daughter with her. "I think it's time we talked about *it*."

Rachel tried to rally her intellect. "It?"

"The daze you've been in. I know it has something to do with the gorgeous guru, since you've been evading him as diligently as you've been deserting reality. What did he do—try to reorganize your brain patterns into neat little rows?"

Rachel laughed, but her heart wasn't in it. She hesitated, then said, "He kissed me. Even worse, I kissed him back.

In fact, we kissed each other like there was no tomorrow."
She sighed. "Except there's always a tomorrow."

"Holy moly! I have to say I wouldn't have thought he
had it in him under all that orderly control, even as attractive as he is. But he obviously does, or you wouldn't be
sitting there looking as if you'd been hit between the eyes."
Bonnie smiled. "And now I'm beginning to understand the
problem. He blew out your circuits. Neil did that the first
time he kissed me. It's not fatal, just debilitating for a
while."

"How long?" Rachel asked, lifting one brow.

Bonnie's smile grew. "I'll let you know when I recover."

It wasn't what Rachel wanted to hear. Yet there didn't
seem to be much she could do about it, she thought glumly,
except perhaps make light of the matter. "I'll triple my
daily dose of vitamin C. Or maybe an enormous bowl of
chicken soup?"

"Chicken soup," a low voice repeated, causing Rachel
to nearly tumble off the stool. The words that followed
were underlined with firm masculine determination.
"Sounds great. I'm getting hungry. Let's go to lunch, Rachel." That's all.

But she also heard, *Your time is up.*

Soon Rachel was seated at a small, umbrella-covered table on the outside rear patio of the English Kitchen, a popular local restaurant. Matthew had acted so quickly and
efficiently that she hadn't had time to think, much less protest, as he'd taken her arm, plucked her from the stool and
marched her out the door, leaving a clearly amused Bonnie
to mind the store.

Rachel slid a glance at the determined man seated opposite her. He was studying a small menu. Once again it
was startlingly apparent to her that Matthew Kent was a
man of action, and, by the rigid set of his jaw, he'd had it

with her efforts to avoid him. People chatted at tables around them, and she wished he would say something; his silence only increased her tension. That was probably his plan, she decided. He'd wait and try to force her to be the first one to speak. *Fat chance.*

"I see they have a Soup of the Day, though it may not be chicken," he said calmly at the very moment she'd convinced herself she was wise to his tactics. "And they have a Miner's Burger, which makes sense. But why the Little Daisy Stuffed Tomato?"

They were going to talk about food titles? Okay, she could play along. "The Little Daisy Mine was one of the richest in Jerome. Huge fortunes were made before it stopped producing."

"And the Cleopatra Pasta Salad?"

"All of this is Mingus Mountain—" she gestured with one hand "—but the area where Jerome was built is Cleopatra Hill."

Their conversation continued in the same vein until a young waiter took their order and departed.

"How did the city itself come to be called Jerome?" Matthew asked, leaning back in his chair. A gentle breeze that kept the air comfortably mild even in August was ruffling his thick black hair.

They were going to discuss local history? All right, she could deal with that. "Eugene Jerome, a wealthy New Yorker, invested in the mining camp on the condition the place be named after him. He was a relative of Jennie Jerome, by the way."

"Jennie Jerome," Matthew repeated thoughtfully. "Sounds familiar for some reason."

"She married Lord Randolph Churchill and had a child by the name of Winston."

"Of course. That guy. An underachiever if there ever was one," he said with a completely deadpan expression.

As he'd done on a few occasions since they'd met, he surprised a laugh out of her. "I'm sure Jennie's son had some redeeming qualities," she said.

Thirty minutes later they were halfway through their lunch and still discussing Jerome and its history. Rachel began to relax and actually taste the Verde Valley Greens salad she'd been forcing down. Because Matthew seemed to be genuinely interested in the topic, she found herself caught up in her enthusiasm for the place she now called home.

"You really like it here," Matthew stated after she'd related another mining story. He was making inroads on his Mingus Mountain Club sandwich.

"I love it," she admitted. "So much that it's hard to imagine living anywhere else now."

"Even after growing up in Tucson and having family there?"

She was surprised he remembered. But she shouldn't be, she reminded herself. This man had a mind capable of storing volumes of data, financial and otherwise, and retrieving it at a moment's notice. She'd already seen evidence of that fact. "Tucson's a beautiful city," she told him, "but I prefer a smaller place. And I see my family a few times a year."

"Tell me about your father…the banker…who's retired."

Matthew saw Rachel go completely still, a forkful of salad halfway to her mouth. He knew he could have gotten the information from Jack; they'd been sharing the second-floor apartment since his uncle's arrival. But he hadn't asked because he wanted to hear whatever there was to hear from Rachel. So he had lulled her with casual conversation until an opportunity had presented itself. He would find out what he wanted to know before they left this table, he vowed, even if he had to pull it out of her word by word.

"Rachel?" he prompted softly, implacably.

Rachel lowered her fork to her plate. When she spoke, her voice was calm and emotionless. "My father, William, plays golf several times a week, and he and my brother are converting a portion of the basement into a woodworking shop. This winter, he's taking my mother on a trip to Hawaii. He seems happy."

"How old is he?"

"Fifty-seven."

"That's rather young to retire, isn't it?"

"In his case, retirement wasn't completely voluntary."

"Why?"

Rachel pushed her plate away and lifted her chin. "What is this—an interrogation?"

Matthew had to admire that gesture of defiance, even though he wouldn't let her get away with it. He set aside his own plate. "Call it anything you like," he told her bluntly, patience gone. "Why did he have to retire, Rachel?"

"Because he had a massive heart attack a year ago."

He didn't know what shook him more, her stark admission or the vivid memory of his own father's appallingly sudden death from exactly the same cause. Still, he couldn't drop the subject. Not now, when he was getting a glimmer of what Jackson McCarthy had referred to, as unwelcome as it appeared to be. "Your father had to quit for health reasons," he summed up, "but he didn't want to...because he liked his work."

Rachel leaned back in her chair and folded her arms under her breasts. "*Like* doesn't even start to cover how my father felt about his work. He was obsessed by it. I can guarantee you that the person who coined the phrase 'banker's hours' never met William Wilson."

Bingo! Matthew thought. He had it now, though it didn't

please him. He frowned. ''And you believe I'm like him,'' he added grimly. It was a statement, not a question.

''I have to admit the thought has crossed my mind.''

''Is that why you've been avoiding me these last few days?''

Rachel just sat there with the warm wind blowing her brown hair over one T-shirt-clad shoulder. The long, shiny strands were held off her face by a large silver clip at the nape of her neck. He had never seen her hair loose and flowing. Maybe he never would. Why did that fill him with such a sense of loss?

''I don't want to get involved with anyone who would put work before everything,'' she said at last, breaking into his thoughts. ''I spent a good portion of my childhood loving a man who had little time for me. There was usually something more important than my birthday party or school play or graduation. He was even late for my wedding.''

I would never treat any child of mine like that, Matthew wanted to say. And couldn't. Because, honestly, he wasn't absolutely sure. He had never had to take time out from his business to deal with the needs of a child.

''It's ironic,'' Rachel continued, ''but now he wants to spend time with me and Tim, my brother. Tim is still young enough—he'll graduate from college next spring—that my father's been able to forge a bond between them. But for me—for *us*—I think it's too late. I'll always love him, yet I'll probably never be close to him.'' There was neither sadness nor regret apparent in her last statement, merely stoic acceptance.

A long silence passed between them before Matthew said, ''Regardless of what you think of me, Rachel, Monday night happened. It's useless to pretend it didn't. The physical attraction's there—whether we want it to be or not.''

She studied him carefully. "You're not so sure about all this yourself, are you?"

Matthew knew she was referring to that attraction. He shook his head. "Quite frankly, you're a witchy woman who scares the hell out of me."

Her startled laugh was brief before her expression sobered once more. "I'm scared, too."

"I know. That, plus my common sense, is the only thing keeping me from pulling you across the table and into my lap right now."

Her eyes widened. "You can't!"

He smiled in spite of himself. "I can...but I won't."

RATHER THAN RETURNING immediately to the store after a lunch neither finished, at Matthew's suggestion they took a walk down Main Street, Jerome's major thoroughfare. In this case, "major" meant a narrow street only several blocks long, and "down" was a literal term. Because Jerome's streets were part of the series of switchback roads climbing the mountain, one had to walk either up or down. They were headed downward. Old two- and three-story homes, now housing businesses that sold everything from art in the form of paintings and sculpture to jewelry to southwestern-style clothing, lined the road.

Interspersed with the stores were small restaurants and a few bars. Country music slipped through the open side door of one of the old-style taverns; the poignant sound of guitars, backing a George Jones rendition of "He Stopped Loving Her Today," swelled as Rachel and Matthew approached a busy corner.

Rachel was still mulling over the scene at the luncheon table. Matthew hadn't denied her implication that work was paramount in his life. Undoubtedly she wouldn't have believed him if he had. From their very first meeting, her instincts had warned her to give him a wide berth. Now, on a conscious level, she realized why. It had been an act of emotional self-preservation. This man could hurt her.

Too bad her body didn't agree with her reasoning processes.

Even now her blood hummed in response to his blunt admission. If he *had* pulled her into his lap…no, she wouldn't think about that. It was much safer not to.

"A place on this street would be an ideal location for a retail business," Matthew said as he studied several groups of shoppers passing them in both directions.

Grateful that he'd chosen an impersonal topic for conversation, Rachel nodded. "It's hard to beat a spot on Main. Visitors immediately head here. A store has to stand out to get their attention if it's on the edge of the shopping area, like the Realm of Romance. That's why the house was painted pink."

Matthew smiled wryly. "You mean it was a logical, rational decision…Rosie?"

"It actually worked, too," she replied with mock solemnity, ignoring his rose-colored-glasses reference. "Business picked up substantially."

His expression turned thoughtful. It was a look she'd observed on more than one occasion since she'd known him. She could almost see columns of numbers forming in his head as he said, "But just think of the possibilities if—"

He broke off as a young man raced out of the side door of the bar they were passing. Following on his heels was a hefty man around forty, dressed from hulking shoulders to booted toes in black leather; even his dusty, battered cowboy hat was black.

Rachel recognized the older man. Little Earl, as he was called, was a burly biker who could usually be found in Jerome on a summer weekend. Although he'd visited her store a few times to buy greeting cards for his mother—

even a man as scruffy-looking as Earl had a mother he obviously cared about—he had never made trouble. Little Earl's natural expression was a bit on the ferocious side, yet Rachel knew he was mild-mannered—except when he'd been drinking heavily. She was afraid this was one of those times, judging by the way he stopped a foot away from her, raised a broad fist and yelled after the young man who was now sprinting down the street as fast as his running shoes could take him.

"Don't you *ever* call George Jones a *has-been,* you moron! He'll still be singin' when you're a grandfather—if I let you live that long." With those ominous words, Little Earl lowered his arm, did a half turn and took one step back toward the tavern. Then he noticed Rachel and a wide grin split his face. "Well, if it ain't the little lady from the row-mance store. Got any row-mance for me today, honey?"

"She doesn't have anything for you," Matthew said calmly as he moved closer to Rachel and took her arm.

The burly man's grin died and his hazel eyes sharpened as he took in Matthew's appearance. "I was talkin' to the lady. Not you, Mr. Businessman."

"The lady's with me," Matthew told him. His voice remained calm and even, but his long fingers tightened their hold on Rachel's arm. "If you'll excuse us?"

Little Earl moved to block Matthew's way. "Well, now, I don't feel like eggs-cusing you. You want to get past, you can climb over me." He spread his arms out from his sides. "And it wouldn't be sportin' to try to walk around me, either."

Matthew studied him. "It appears we have a problem, Mr.—?"

"Little Earl Dobbs."

"Mr. Dobbs. It could be easily solved by stepping aside."

Little Earl's grin returned. He was clearly enjoying himself. "Uh-uh. You'll have to move me...if you can."

Matthew let his breath out in a resigned sigh. He released his hold on Rachel's arm and looked down at her. "I want you to go back to the store. I'll be along shortly."

"Yeah, somebody'll be carrying him," Little Earl said with a deep chuckle that approached a growl.

Rachel ignored him and stared at her companion. "You're going to fight him, aren't you?" She didn't wait for an answer; the truth was evident in the steady, uncompromising look in his eyes. "This is ridiculous!"

He frowned at her. "Sometimes these things can't be avoided, Rachel. Please go home."

She frowned back at him. "I will *not* go home."

"Eggs-cuse me," Little Earl said with exaggerated courtesy, "but can we get on with this? I've got a mug of beer waitin'."

Matthew continued as if the other man hadn't spoken. "If you won't go home, then stand there—" he put a hand in the small of her back and nudged her "—by the side of the building."

She wanted to argue. "Matthew—"

"Now." It was a command, pure and simple.

Because she knew he was concerned for her safety, she swallowed her irritation and did as he said. For the first time she noticed a small crowd had gathered, although no one was getting too close. She couldn't stop what was about to happen, she realized. Even if she ran to a phone and called the police, by the time they got there it would probably be over.

She was proved right when events proceeded very quickly.

Little Earl threw a weighty punch and wound up sprawled out on the sidewalk seconds later. Matthew had moved with stunning effectiveness to accomplish that.

When Earl rebounded, punches two and three produced exactly the same result.

After landing on his back for the fourth time, Little Earl just lay there obviously dazed by the speed and skill of his opponent. Almost as amazing as Matthew's completely unexpected martial-arts expertise was the fact that Little Earl's black hat had stayed firmly in place throughout all the tumbles he'd taken. And even more astonishing was the total absence of the remarkable temper Rachel had once witnessed in Matthew. This time, he remained coolly in control of himself and the situation.

He hadn't remained unscathed, however. His white shirt was torn at one shoulder, and Little Earl had managed to graze his jaw with one punch. Still, clearly he was the victor. Taking a deep breath, he hunkered down by the side of his fallen adversary. "Are we done, Dobbs?" he asked in the same calm tone he'd used before the altercation.

As the crowd drifted away, the prostrate man raised himself up on his elbows. "Anyone who can beat me can call me Little Earl. How the hell did you do that?"

"It's something I learned in the Orient—a discipline that channels the power of the mind and the body. Staying focused is the key, Little Earl, and too much alcohol muddles the brain." He extended his right hand. "I'm Matthew Kent, by the way."

Little Earl smiled as they shook hands. "You're right. I did have a drop too much, but you sobered me up real quick. Might've even done me a favor. Some of my bonus money might actually be left when the weekend's over. 'Scuse the ruckus."

Matthew gave him a long, hard look. "Ms. McCarthy's the one who deserves an apology."

"Sorry, Miz McCarthy," Little Earl said with an obviously contrite expression on his face.

Rachel nodded her acceptance and walked toward them. Both men got to their feet and brushed themselves off.

"What business are you in?" Matthew asked, tucking his shirt into the waistband of his gray wool pants.

"I'm a trucker," Little Earl replied, and identified a well-known firm as his employer. "I make a long haul every week to the Midwest, so I like to ride up here and relax on the weekends." He straightened his leather jacket. "I've been known to relax too much when I get a bonus for an extra-fast delivery."

"You work hard to make a living. Why don't you try putting some of that bonus money to work for you?"

Little Earl's hazel eyes sharpened again, this time with curiosity. "What you do mean?"

Rachel watched in fascination as the discussion that followed ranged from certificates of deposit to money-market options to individual retirement accounts. She'd witnessed male bonding before, but this took the cake! What had started out as a fight had turned into a financial seminar right before her eyes. After exchanging phone numbers, the two men shook hands again.

"Thanks for the advice, Mr. Kent. I'll look into it."

"It's Matthew, and if you've got more questions, call me."

"I'll do it. And if I can ever do anything for *you,* just holler. A man never knows when he might need a friend."

Walking back to the store with a quiet Rachel at his side, Matthew considered the burly man's departing words. He didn't have any friends. Not *real* friends. He used to, but somehow he'd lost touch with them as he became increasingly involved in his work. Why had he let that happen? he asked himself as he touched his jaw gingerly. It was still sore from Little Earl's punch. Strange, he hadn't considered that lack of genuine friendship before today. Then again, he hadn't had much time for contemplation. Until he came to Jerome.

LATE THE NEXT AFTERNOON Matthew climbed the stairs to the second-floor apartment. A light, fragrant rain fell softly to mingle with a dense blanket of cloudy mist covering the green valley far below. He'd spent most of the day in the office, entering inventory data into the computer. That particular portion of the project was nearly finished. What would he do with himself when the new system was up and running? It would take perhaps another week to accomplish that at the rate he was going, and he still had four weeks to spend here.

He hadn't seen much of Rachel since they'd returned from their lunch yesterday. Clearly she was avoiding him again. She didn't want to—or was she afraid to?—get involved with him. Now that he knew something of her childhood and her father, he understood one reason for her wariness. In fact, he had a hard time disagreeing with it, at least on a rational level.

Too bad his body had decided to go its own way.

Regardless of the fact that she did absolutely nothing to try to attract him, she attracted him. He'd discovered over the past week that an oversize T-shirt could well be the most erotic garment known to man. It wasn't what it revealed—it was what it concealed. He was going crazy imagining what was under it.

And no matter how much he told himself she was the wrong woman for him, he wanted her. He'd even dreamed about her the night before. In his arms. In his bed. Long, shining hair spread over his pillow. He'd woken breathing hard, fully aroused…and achingly unsatisfied. At this very moment his mutinous body was responding again, just from the memory.

Matthew issued a succinct curse and gritted his teeth. He

opened the apartment door and slammed it shut behind him. Hodgepodge welcomed him as if he'd been gone for a decade. He took time to crouch down for a moment and rub the soft skin behind the dog's floppy ears. "At least *you're* always glad to see me, mutt," he said under his breath. Then, getting a whiff of what was undoubtedly his uncle's latest culinary effort, he straightened and walked into the kitchen. The food situation was the one thing that had improved dramatically during the past week.

Dressed in his usual khaki, Jackson McCarthy stood at the stove, browning chicken pieces in a sizzling skillet. He slanted an appraising glance at his nephew. "You look like you're ready to swallow nails. The vacation must be getting to you." Abandoning the chicken, he began to slice an onion. "I asked Rachel to come for dinner. Actually, I demanded her presence. She's been spending too many evenings by herself—although her apartment's a pleasant place. Nice and cozy, don't you think?"

"I wouldn't know," Matthew growled.

"So you haven't been invited up to the ivory tower."

He ignored his uncle's wry comment.

"The weather's supposed to clear tomorrow," Jack continued. "I'm going fishing for a couple of days. Want to join me?"

Matthew leaned against the refrigerator and crossed his arms over his chest. He had a vague recollection of a fishing trip when he was a boy. Not with his father, of course; Andrew Kent would have been much too busy. Probably he had tagged along with the family of one of his friends. He couldn't remember if he'd enjoyed it, but he had no desire to do it now. "Thanks, but I'll stay here."

Jack shrugged. "Suit yourself. You'd better do something, though, to unwind." He threw the sliced onion in with the chicken and gave it a practiced stir. "Maybe I should teach you to cook. It can be soothing. Even if it doesn't work and you're still climbing the walls, you'll be eating better in the future than you were when I got here." He retrieved a colander filled with artichoke hearts from its place by the sink. "I'm making Chicken Bordelaise. It's not too difficult. Want to try?"

Because his frustration level compelled him to do something—*anything*—to keep occupied, Matthew nodded grimly. "I'll take a chance, if you will."

Jack's brown eyes lit with amusement. "It's only a meal, Matt, not the fate of the Western world. Relax. I'll explain what to do."

Twenty minutes later Jack sampled the simmering contents of the skillet. "This is good...as good as I've ever made." There was a hint of astonishment in that statement.

Matthew braced one hip against the counter and took a sip of the white wine his uncle had poured. "You were the one calling the shots."

"No, it's more than that." Jack stroked his dark beard thoughtfully. "The same dish can be made in exactly the same manner, yet it's the cook who determines the final outcome. Don't ask me why, but it's something in the touch that separates the adequate from the excellent. You might have it." All at once he started to pace rapidly back and forth, his customary indolence gone. Then he came to an abrupt halt and raised his long wooden spoon like a soldier wielding a sword in battle. "Let's make some soufflés!"

Even with his extremely limited knowledge regarding the mechanics of haute cuisine, Matthew knew how difficult a soufflé was. "You're out of your mind!"

His uncle was already bending to get a carton of eggs from the refrigerator. "We'll each make a soufflé for dessert while the chicken is finishing." Swiftly, he pulled other ingredients from a cabinet. "I bought some Grand Marnier the other day. It'll add a great orange flavor."

Matthew soon gave up protesting and with Jack's guidance started to separate eggs into two bowls. It appeared the only way to convince Jack of the futility of this experiment was to go through with it. He resigned himself to the inevitable and did as his uncle directed.

In no time at all, or so it seemed to Matthew because he'd been concentrating intently on his task, two high, round baking dishes containing egg mixtures prepared separately by teacher and pupil were placed on the middle rack of a hot oven.

When a knock sounded on the outside door, Jack polished off his wine and went to answer it. He greeted Rachel with a wily grin. "Glad you could make it."

Rachel found herself grinning in response, though earlier she'd been mightily annoyed at Jack's high-handed insistence that she come for dinner. But then, he'd always been able to charm her, right from the very first day she'd met him years earlier.

"We've got a surprise for you." Jack took her arm and led her into the kitchen.

Rachel gazed at the disaster awaiting her. Pots and pans filled the sink and covered the countertops. "If the surprise is that I get to do all the dishes, I'm going to run back out the door."

Chuckling, Jack escorted her past the chaos and into the dining room. Matthew stood there, setting the table. Rachel smothered her own chuckle when she saw him placing silverware next to white dinner plates with absolute precision. God help the knife or fork that strayed a millimeter from its assigned position, she thought.

"The surprise," Jack said as he poured her a glass of wine, "is that Matt made Chicken Bordelaise, and it's going to be delicious." With those words, he returned to the kitchen.

Matthew courteously pulled out a chair; Rachel sank into

it. "I'm more than surprised—I'm amazed." She looked at him over her shoulder. "I thought you couldn't cook."

He shook his head and sat down beside her. "I can't. It's a figment of Jack's imagination. He told me what to do and I did it, that's all."

Jack brought in a steaming platter heaped high with chicken and vegetables and set it in the middle of the table. Using a large ladle, he began to serve generous portions. Rachel hadn't seen or smelled food as good as this for some time, since she wasn't much of a cook herself.

Jack took the chair across from her. "I think Matt's underestimating his abilities, but tonight's dessert will tell the tale."

She groaned. "Jack, you didn't...?"

His smile told its own tale. "*We* did."

Noting Matthew's puzzled expression, she explained, "Jack and I made soufflés once. His was a glorious creation. Mine, however, flattened like a pancake when it came out of the oven."

Matthew grimaced. "Mine's bound to be worse."

But when the baking dishes were carefully removed and placed on the counter a half hour later, both desserts stood straight and tall. Rachel watched in bemusement as uncle grabbed nephew in a brief, bruising hug. "Well, I'll be damned. You've got flair, Matt! *Flair*. And you must have gotten it from me, because no one else in the family has it." He hugged Matthew again. "I'll be damned," Jack repeated dazedly.

Matthew looked at Rachel over his uncle's shoulder. He appeared a little dazed himself. "I've got flair," he told her.

And then he began to laugh. It was low and somewhat rusty, yet it was definitely a laugh. She realized it was the first time she'd heard that sound from him. How long had it been since he had really all-out laughed?

The soufflés tasted as good as they looked. Everyone agreed on that—even Hodgepodge, whose small serving quickly disappeared.

Rachel sighed contentedly. "That was even more wonderful than the chicken. If there weren't all those dishes in the sink, things would be perfect." She pushed back her chair. "We'd better get started on them. And speaking of kitchen sinks, mine's leaking again, Jack. Can you take a look at it after we're through here?" She rose and stacked the dessert plates.

If Matthew hadn't chosen that exact moment to look at his uncle, he would have missed the speculative glance tossed his way. An instant later, Jack said, "My back's been bothering me. I don't think it would be a good idea to try to fit myself under a sink. Matt will take care of it."

For some reason, Jack had decided to give him this opportunity, Matthew realized. He knew less than nothing about plumbing, but he was a man who took advantage of opportunities. When Rachel's mouth opened—to protest, he was certain—he cut her off. "I'll be glad to do what I can," he said smoothly as he got to his feet, hoping there was something he *could* do.

Jack's wily grin appeared. "Good. My toolbox is in the closet in my bedroom. You'll find everything you need."

Matthew merely nodded once in reply. Just like that, he'd won admittance to Rachel's apartment—the "ivory tower."

6

"YOU CAN DO THIS, Kent," Matthew muttered under his breath as he wedged his broad shoulders through the opening of the cabinet under the sink. A drop of water smacked his forehead.

Rachel stood next to the sink. All he could see of her were canvas shoes and the lower half of denim-covered legs. "Can you tell where it's leaking?"

He pushed in farther; another drop plopped on his nose. Looking up, he saw moisture beading at a joint where the pipe curved. "I found it." Now all he had to do was stop it...somehow. "Would you move the toolbox closer?"

Rachel complied. "Anything else I can do?"

The last thing he needed was an audience. "Uh-uh. Everything's under control."

"Are you sure?" she asked doubtfully.

"I'm positive." It was a firm statement.

"Okay, I'll be in the living room." With that, she turned and walked away.

Hodgepodge poked his furry head through the opening.

"Do you have any plumbing experience, mutt?" An ardent panting started. "Well, you probably know as much about it as I do, but I'll get this damn thing fixed one way or the other."

Whatever he was going to do, he wanted to get it over with and join Rachel. Logically he knew that was a bad idea. He was already having erotic dreams about her; he didn't need to spend more time with her. He wanted to anyway. So much for logic.

And now he'd be able to envision where she lived, Matthew thought, reaching under one of the dog's long ears to pull a wrench from a gray metal box. The third-floor apartment, or as much of it as he'd seen so far, resembled the one below even beyond its configuration. Rachel, too, apparently preferred lace curtains and cotton fabrics—that fact didn't surprise him—but where the second-floor flat was arrayed predominantly in bright shades of yellow and red, in this one the colors were darker—rich burgundies and deep greens. He would have guessed her tastes ranged more to dusky pinks and cool blues.

Abruptly the boisterous sound of Bruce Springsteen reminiscing about "Glory Days" pulsed down the hall from the living room. Rock and roll rather than violins? That was one more surprise. Yet another drop of water struck his chin. It was time to get on with it. "You can do this, Kent."

Rachel winced, hearing the piercing clash of metal meeting metal over the music she'd switched on moments before. Did he really know what he was doing? she wondered. Well, it was too late to worry about it now. It would be more constructive to worry about what she'd do with him when he was through. She couldn't just show him to the door. She didn't want him here, but he was here, and she would have to be hospitable.

Resolving to tune out the clatter emanating from the kitchen, Rachel settled back on the sofa and picked up a half-finished novel. She read twenty pages without retaining a single word before Matthew appeared in the doorway to the hall. And what a sight he was.

He looked as if he'd been fighting a flood.

His dark hair, flecked with moisture, hung down over his forehead. His white shirt, so pristine just minutes ago, was spotted with water and specks of dirt. The sharp creases in his navy wool pants had given up the battle and wilted. Even the dog standing at his side had a wet face and two damp, droopy ears.

She had to bite her tongue to thwart a laugh. She knew when male pride was on the line. "All done?" she asked as calmly as she could manage.

Matthew nodded gravely in reply.

"There are plenty of towels in the bathroom if you'd like to clean up."

Man and dog left her, but both were back moments later. Although they still looked somewhat bedraggled, at least they were drier. It was time to be the gracious hostess. "Please sit down. Would you like some coffee? Or maybe a brandy?"

Matthew sat on the overstuffed chair across from her; Hodgepodge reclined on the carpet. "A brandy sounds good."

She'd get his brandy, make small talk while he finished it, and send him on his way, she decided as she rose and headed for the kitchen. That was still her plan when she returned, crystal snifter in hand, and found him studying a box she'd set on the floor by the stereo that afternoon.

"'Ports of Pleasure,'" he read out loud, his head slanted to the side, "'a Romantic Voyage of Discovery for Two.'" He turned to her with a quizzical look.

She gave him the glass. "That's one of those games I told you I was considering stocking. I ordered a sample to see what it's like. It came in this morning."

"Have you looked at it yet?"

"I've read the instructions on the back of the box. It seems to fit in with our other merchandise—might even be a big seller. I'll check it out later." She started toward the sofa.

"Why don't we do it now?"

She spun around. "*You* want to look at a romance game?"

Shrugging lightly, he lifted the snifter to his mouth. "If it has promising profit potential, I'd be interested."

That she could believe. If cross-eyed mules had promising profit potential, he'd no doubt be interested. "All right, let's check it out." Might as well examine the game. It would give them something to do until she could get rid of him.

And she *did* want to get rid of him, she assured herself as she took a few steps to the stereo and sat down on the forest-green carpet next to the game box. Still, a tiny, treacherous part of her relished the sight of him seated in her living room. Even damp and rumpled—or maybe because for once he didn't look so totally in control—Matthew Kent was more attractive than any man had a right to be. Much too attractive...to her.

Rachel nudged that thought aside and pulled several items from the box: a game board that opened to reveal a global map with a twisting, checkerboard path connecting several exotic islands and port cities; two tiny glass ships—one white, one black—to be used as playing pieces; a small deck of cards labeled "Wisdom" on one side and listing questions and answers on the other; a similar set of cards labeled "Truth;" and a handful of small, printed vouchers marked "Lover's Reward." Also included were a cassette tape and a pair of dice.

"The object of the game," she explained, "is to move a ship around the globe using the dice. When you land on a Wisdom square, your partner takes a card and reads a question regarding an island or port city. If you answer correctly, you keep the card. After you accumulate three cards, you can trade them in for a reward voucher. When you land on a Truth square, you have to honestly answer whatever question is listed on the card. You can refuse, but if you do, you forfeit whatever Wisdom cards you have at that point and start over. First person to accumulate five reward vouchers wins the game."

Matthew moved to sit cross-legged on the carpet. The game board was between them. "What's the cassette for?"

"It's mood music." She read the label. "'Ocean Sounds for a Rapturous Journey.'"

He raised an eyebrow. "You're kidding."

"Uh-uh. This game is for lovers, remember? *Not* Monopoly."

"All right, let's try it out."

Rachel blinked, feeling as if she'd been whacked over the head with the game board. "You want to *play?*"

The look he gave her was inscrutable; she could well believe he'd spent time in the Orient. "How else can we conduct a meaningful analysis?"

How else indeed? she thought dazedly.

WHY THE DEVIL did you suggest this, Kent? Matthew asked himself that question as he collected his second blue Wisdom card and listened to waves breaking with a languorous, steady beat from the stereo speaker a foot away. Not that he didn't already know the answer. The game was absolute nonsense, but it had provided a very effective excuse to prolong his visit with the woman who was moving her little white ship down the board four spaces. She was stretched out on her side, with an arm bent to cup her chin in the palm of one hand.

"Good, I'm on Truth," she said. "Now we can see what those cards are like." She had already earned one Wisdom card with the correct answer to a question on Hawaii.

He picked the top card from a short purple stack on one side of the board. "Truth be told," he read, "what was your first thought on waking up today?" And thank God he hadn't gotten that one, he reflected, remembering his heated thoughts and his body's fully aroused state when he'd woken that morning.

"I was glad to hear the rain drumming on the roof," Rachel answered promptly. "It's been dry too long."

No erotic dreams? he wanted to ask. And didn't. Instead, he said, "How do we know when the other person is telling the truth?"

"It's the honor system, I guess, since it's not mentioned in the instructions. We'll just have to take it on trust, although I suppose two people involved in an intimate relationship would have a better feel for it."

Matthew threw the dice and moved his black ship six spaces. "Another Wisdom."

Rachel picked up a card. "What is the name of the colorful wrap-around dress worn by the women of Tahiti?"

"A pareo," he replied, without even having to consider it; he'd once removed one of those garments. Yet it hadn't been as enticing as the coral-colored T-shirt worn by the woman across from him that proclaimed A Dose Of Affection Is Good For What Ails You. He was ailing—for more than affection. *Blast it.*

"Pareo's right." She handed him the card. "That gives you three Wisdom cards. You can trade them in for a reward voucher."

He tossed his cards aside, picked up a bright red Lover's Reward slip and turned it over. It was bordered with small gold figures of a male and female in an amorous embrace. "This voucher," he read, "is good for one breakfast in bed…and the dessert of your choice." He shot a glance at Rachel. "What time are you serving, Rosie?"

She frowned back at him. "In case you've forgotten, this is merely an analysis."

"No breakfast?"

"Right."

"And no dessert."

"You got it."

As the game continued, Matthew quickly took the lead. He had traveled all over the world and knew more than a little about a great many places. Before long, he had earned his second reward voucher. Not that he would get *any* lascivious rewards from his playing partner, he thought as he took another turn and landed on a Truth square for the first time.

Rachel read the card. "Truth be told, how do you feel about the day-to-day aspects of marriage?"

Momentarily startled, he remained silent. He didn't have to answer, he knew. But one thing he had always prided himself on was his sense of honesty.

"I suppose that would be a difficult question for a person who's never been married," she added.

"I was married."

Now Rachel was clearly the startled one. Her lips parted, then snapped together.

"It was several years ago," he continued, "shortly after I got out of college. It didn't last very long."

"I'm sorry." There was undeniable sincerity in that soft statement.

He shook his head. "Don't be. Melinda and I have fared much better without each other. She has three children now from her second marriage, which seems to be a happy one. I still get a card from her at Christmas."

Another silent moment, broken only by the sound of the waves, passed before Rachel said, "Do you mind if I ask what she was like?"

He uncrossed his long legs and angled them out to the side. "She was an optimist, idealistic." *Like you.* "She believed in starry-eyed love and happily-ever-after." *Like you.* "We were total opposites." *Like you and me.* "As to the day-to-day aspects of that marriage, they consisted more and more of my losing my temper and her weeping and locking herself in the bedroom. It was a relief when it was over—for both of us.'' He paused. ''That's the truth…and it's your turn to roll the dice.''

But Rachel was still trying to assimilate what he'd revealed. Obviously Matthew had chosen a wife who couldn't deal with her volatile husband, and they had probably been too young to overcome the formidable differences he'd mentioned. Would her own marriage have been as happy if she and Danny had been so totally different, instead of the pals they'd always been?

''Rachel?'' Matthew prompted.

Hauling her thoughts back to the matter at hand, she threw the dice and landed on a Wisdom block.

''Who were the famed lovers associated with the ancient city of Troy?'' he read.

''Helen and Paris.'' With that correct answer, she earned her first Lover's Reward and picked up a red slip. ''This voucher is good for the night of your wildest dreams.''

''What would that night be like?'' he asked in a deep, suddenly intent voice.

Green eyes met steel-gray ones. The conversation had moved far beyond the game, she realized. She searched for a casual response to a question that had been anything *but* casual; it was a futile effort. What kind of night would fulfill her wildest dreams? Completely unbidden, a breathtakingly vivid image of herself locked in Matthew Kent's arms flashed through her mind. Good grief, she couldn't tell him that! ''The rules don't require me to answer,'' was the only reply she could muster.

''As you choose,'' he said smoothly. ''I could describe *my* version.''

''No, that's okay,'' she assured him hastily. She was flustered and knew it was all too evident. ''Just…roll the dice. It's your turn.''

For the first time since he'd entered her living room,

Matthew smiled. He wasn't a man who smiled often; perhaps that was why his wide, genuine grin jostled her pulse and jangled her nerve endings. Silently he launched the dice and wound up on another Truth square.

She selected a purple card, but didn't look at the question. All at once there was something she *had* to ask. She raised her gaze to his. "Truth be told, what do you want from me?"

It was a mistake.

She understood that the instant his gray eyes turned to smoke. One second stretched to five before he said, "This." Just one husky word. Then strong arms reached out to grasp her around the waist, and game cards scattered haphazardly as he pulled her right across the board. Almost before she realized it, they were lying side by side on the carpet, facing each other.

"And this," he murmured, bringing her even closer until only their clothing separated their bodies. She felt his muscled chest against her breasts, his metal belt buckle against her stomach, his rigid arousal against her abdomen, his long legs along the length of hers. He was totally, awesomely male against her female form.

"And most definitely this." His voice was so low, it was almost a growl. Then his lips met hers.

Once again, the staggering impact of his kiss flowed through her in a torrent of emotion, sweeping away resistance before it could take hold. Again, she closed her eyes and was swamped by pleasure as he thrust his tongue into her mouth. It was an invasion, pure and simple. She understood that. What she couldn't begin to understand was the fact that she welcomed it. Why was she welcoming this man who could hurt her?

And then he groaned in the back of his throat and deepened the kiss and understanding anything was far beyond her. Instinctively she wrapped her arms around his neck and was swiftly engulfed by the potent tide of longing he created inside her. It was every bit as powerful, and as mesmerizing, as the ocean waves that still pounded forcefully somewhere in the background. She was submerged in the tangy, brandy-edged taste, the musky male smell, the vitally masculine feel of him. Drowning in him…and going down for the third time with no thought to save herself.

Once again, Matthew relished the freshness of Rachel's response. This time, it sparked a hunger that sent one large hand in a resolute quest over her body before he even considered the wisdom of that action. He had certainly felt sexual craving before, yet the fierceness of *this* hunger staggered him. It was an unexpected and very formidable menace to his self-control. He realized that. What he couldn't fathom was his willingness to proceed in spite of it. He was a smart man; it was a dumb thing to do. He wanted to, anyway. So much for intelligence.

She has to be a green-eyed witch, he thought as he savored a warm, moist mouth and stroked long fingers over her cotton T-shirt. An instant later he found what he sought—what he *had* to touch: an oh-so-soft breast large enough to more than fill his greedy palm. Gently he squeezed, and the woman in his arms pressed closer. It was an irresistible invitation he immediately accepted by slipping his hand under her shirt to feel the satiny skin of her stomach, then the wispy lace of her bra.

Growing more aroused by the second, Matthew pushed one hard thigh between Rachel's legs as he brushed his thumb over a lace-covered nipple. Instantly she drew her mouth from his and gasped in reaction, but her eyes remained closed.

"Do you like that?"

After a heartbeat's hesitation, she murmured her assent so quietly he could scarcely hear it.

"This—" he flecked his finger over the stiffening peak

"—or this?" He began to move his leg slowly back and forth between supple thighs in a blatantly intimate caress.

"Every..." She took a deep breath. "Everything."

He couldn't suppress a sudden smile steeped in male satisfaction, although he'd been prepared for that response. Other women had responded in exactly the same way. What surprised him was his own unprecedented reaction. He wanted to strip Rachel bare and take her now, on the floor, right on top of the game board, without a trace of his usual practiced finesse. He wanted to play a wild, lusty and far more exciting game than the one they'd just played—a contest they could both win while they lost themselves in each other. His body clamored for it. For her. He was at the very limits of his self-control.

Then the steady sound of breaking waves ceased with a sharp click as the tape ended.

Rachel's eyes popped open.

Watching her intently in the suddenly taut silence, Matthew nearly groaned in frustration when he saw sparks of passion being squelched by doubts. He could rekindle the blaze, he knew, but he had regained a margin of his control...along with his own doubts. What the devil was he doing, making love to this woman—the wrong kind of woman? Except she felt *right*. Dammit.

He forced his hand from her breast and slowly removed his leg from between hers. "You asked for the truth," he reminded her, his voice low and husky, "but I think things got a little out of hand." And *that* had to be the understatement of the year.

He saw disappointment mingled with relief in her expression as she sat up and straightened her clothing. She wanted him, all right, yet not enough to overcome her misgivings. Perhaps it was just as well. And if he repeated that to himself a hundred times—preferably while taking an ice-cold shower—he might begin to believe it.

Rachel cleared her throat. "Yes, things did…get out of hand. It must have been the game—all that romance."

If she wanted to believe that, he'd let her, but he was positive the outcome would have been the same if they'd been playing checkers. Stiffly he got to his feet and noted her gaze slide over the front of his pants as it climbed to his face. He couldn't hide his condition and didn't much care if the woman with the rose-colored view of the world saw it. His arousal was stark reality. "I'd better be going," he said. *Otherwise, I may just bury those doubts and take up where we left off.*

She rose to stand next to him. "Thanks for your help with my plumb—" She came to a dead stop, clearly perceiving there could be a double meaning in that statement. "I mean…thanks."

"You're quite welcome," he replied dryly. Then he glanced down at the sleepy dog sprawled on the carpet. "Come on, mutt, it's time to go."

FIFTEEN MINUTES LATER Matthew entered the second floor apartment. He'd spent most of those minutes contemplating the dark valley beyond the back porch railing and had made a decision. He had to put some distance between himself and Rachel McCarthy, and one way to accomplish that had become apparent. Yes, it would serve the purpose, Matthew reflected as he found his uncle in the kitchen, leaning against the counter and finishing another helping of soufflé.

Jack grinned his wily grin. "All fixed?"

"It's fixed," Matthew told him grimly. "When do we leave on our fishing trip?"

"Changed your mind, did you?" Jack's grin widened when Matthew remained silent. He knew his sexual frustration must be evident to the older man. "Well, tomorrow morning's fine with me," Jack continued. "Just pack some old, beat-up clothes and a pair of boots. I've got enough other gear for the both of us.''

"This is as beat-up as it gets.'' Matthew indicated the shirt and pants he wore.

Jack lifted a brow. "Good God, Matt. Don't you even own a pair of jeans?''

"No.''

Shaking his head in resignation, Jack said, "If you didn't have flair, I'd be inclined to think there was no hope for you. We'll stop somewhere along the way and you can buy some stuff. The fish would laugh themselves to death if you tried to catch anything wearing that Brooks Brothers outfit.''

Matthew didn't care what the hell he wore. He just needed to get out of Jerome.

RACHEL STOOD at one of the third-floor front windows, still dressed in her nightgown and white terry-cloth robe, and watched them load up Jack's ancient, mud-green Jeep on Monday morning. They had stopped by minutes before to tell her about their trip. Or, rather, Jack had told her, chatting breezily as Hodgepodge gave her hand a goodbye flick with a rough, moist tongue. Matthew had merely watched her with an imperturbable calmness, giving no clue as to his thoughts or feelings.

She was glad he was going, she told herself. She desperately needed some time away from him after last night's events. She hadn't slept a wink. Throughout the endless night, every single, sleep-defying minute of it as she lay in bed, she'd remembered his kiss. And much more. The electrifying feel of his large hand on her breast and his hard thigh between hers. The breathtaking sight of his undeniable arousal. Everything.

He had wanted her. And she had wanted him.

The Jeep, now laden with all the equipment the male of

the species deemed necessary for a fishing expedition, pulled away from the curb and Rachel turned from the window. They were on their way. Maybe tonight she would be able to sleep, knowing Matthew wasn't in the bedroom one floor below her. Maybe.

"You have to get a grip, Rach," she ordered sternly as she sat on the sofa. She took a sip of her second cup of coffee and set it aside. "So he kissed you. So you kissed him. So he made you feel things you've never felt before…glorious things."

She closed her eyes and sighed. There was still a mountain of uncertainties between them—on both sides, she knew by his wary expression when he'd left last night. She had to put things in perspective before he returned. She had to.

The telephone shrilled. She picked it up on the third ring and swallowed a sudden urge to yawn. "Hello."

A soft yet extremely efficient female voice said, "May I please speak to Rachel McCarthy."

"Speaking."

"Ms. McCarthy, this is Cynthia Renault from the Morgan Agency in New York City. I'm delighted to tell you that…."

As the voice went on, Rachel's jaw dropped and her eyes widened in shock.

"I'M GOING TO have the bastard for dinner if it's the last thing I ever do," Matthew vowed, casting his fishing line from the banks of the Verde River with far more determination than expertise. His hair hung down over his forehead, his nose was sunburned, his hands were grubby, and a short layer of dark stubble had sprouted on his chin and jaw. He wore snug-fitting Levi's, a blue denim shirt, and tan boots that were still damp from an earlier dunking in clear, cold water.

"It might well be the last thing you do if you fall in one more time and get pneumonia," Jack replied dryly, standing next to him. "That shrewd old catfish has been toying with you for the past two days. Why don't you try for some smallmouth bass? They're better eating, anyway."

Matthew shook his head stubbornly. "It's become a personal vendetta. I'm sick and tired of losing bait to the son of a—" All at once his line went taut. "I've got him now."

"That's what you said the last time," Jack reminded him. "And the time before that. And the time before that."

Matthew ignored those wry words and carefully edged closer to the water, making sure to keep his line tight as he slowly reeled it in.

Hodgepodge growled in encouragement. At least Matthew took it that way. "I know *you* have faith in me, mutt. All I have to do is wear the rascal down and—" Suddenly the fish started to swim straight toward him until it was only a few feet away, then it headed off to the right, the hook still in its mouth. Matthew followed doggedly, sprinting in an effort to keep the line taut. To the right. Then to the left. Then to the right again. Until the fish headed farther out. And swiftly back again.

It went on for the better part of an hour, and at one point Matthew once again wound up in frigid, knee-high water.

But this time Kent determination to succeed won the day. And the cunning catfish. Hodgepodge barked enthusiastically when Matthew finally reeled it in.

Jack's huge grin held a hint of pride as he considered his nephew. "Congratulations, Matt." He slapped him on the back. "It's a great catch—must be at least ten pounds. Although the bugger might be too mean to eat."

Matthew studied the large fish still wiggling tenaciously on the hook. "The hell it is," he decreed. "We're eating it."

They ate it, coated lightly with cornmeal and fried over

the small campsite fire. It was one of the best meals he'd ever had, Matthew reflected with satisfaction as he got into his sleeping bag that night and looked up at an awesome display of stars. He took a deep breath of cool, crisp air. The majesty of the great outdoors. He hadn't experienced it often.

The trip was going well—much better than he'd expected. It would have been even more enjoyable if he'd been able to forget Rachel. Forget what had happened between them. Forget his hunger for her. But he couldn't forget.

"Do you want to head back to Jerome tomorrow or stay another day?" Jack asked. He was in his own sleeping bag a few feet away. Hodgepodge was stretched out between them.

Matthew spied the Big Dipper. "It's up to you."

"Let's move down the river, then, and stay until Thursday morning. Maybe we can find another stubborn catfish for you to duel with." Jack chuckled. "It was a great day. My only regret is that your father couldn't see you in action—although he'd probably want to yank out my liver for taking you on such a frivolous expedition. No business strategy being developed. No profit being made. He'd have narrowed his gray eyes at that."

Even though he knew it was true, that statement irritated Matthew. The man they were discussing had, after all, fathered him; he felt compelled to defend Andrew Kent. "I know the two of you didn't get along, Jack. But my father worked hard, he was an honorable man and raised me as best he could."

Jack's low voice took on an edge of grimness. "He didn't do his best—not by a long shot. Unfortunately I'm just beginning to realize it."

"What's that supposed to mean?" Matthew raised himself up on his elbows to peer at his uncle through the dimness.

Jack gazed up at the sky and cursed softly and at length. ''Nothing. Forget it,'' he muttered at last. ''Let's get some sleep.'' Abruptly he turned over and gave his pillow a swift, forceful punch.

What had all that been about? Matthew wondered as he lay back and laced his fingers behind his head. Finally he decided to take Jack's advice and forget it. The past was just that—past. Tomorrow, they'd go fishing again and he'd enjoy this time with his uncle. At least as much as he could when he knew he had to return to Jerome and the sweet torture of being around Rachel.

He could still envision her as she'd looked on Monday morning, dusky circles under her eyes from an obviously sleepless night and wrapped in that old terry-cloth robe. It was one of the least provocative garments he'd ever viewed on a woman. But now, though he hadn't actually seen them, he knew that under that robe *this woman's breasts were* full and soft and... He gritted his teeth to stifle a groan. He was going to drive himself crazy with that line of thinking. Yet her choice of clothing intrigued him. A practical cotton T-shirt concealing that totally impractical wisp of lace. What had she been wearing under those jeans?

When his groin tightened in response to a vivid image of supple hips encased in skimpy silk, Matthew turned over and punched his own pillow in frustration. *You're not winning this battle, Kent.* He sighed gustily as he finally admitted defeat. The green-eyed witch had cast a spell too strong to be broken. She might be the wrong kind of woman, but it didn't matter. He had to have Rachel McCarthy as his lover, and he would set about accomplishing that when he got back to Jerome.

For the second time that day, Matthew Kent became a very determined man.

SOMETHING WAS UP. Matthew came to that conclusion moments after Jack braked the old Jeep to a stop in front of the store late Thursday afternoon. Through the display window he saw Rachel behind the counter, surrounded by several Jerome store owners he'd met during his stay. All he could recall were first names. Diana and Dolores were partners in Double D Designs, a trendy Southwestern clothing store. Ann had a small art gallery nearby. And Darlene owned the chocolate shop, Sweet Temptation. The group, which included Bonnie Gallico, laughed and waved hands in the air. Darlene jumped up and down like a schoolgirl.

Something was definitely up.

Entering the store minutes later, Hodgepodge at his side, Matthew carried a duffel bag and several pieces of fishing gear. Jack, similarly burdened, brought up the rear.

"And the most amazing thing is that it could happen so quickly," Bonnie was saying, her back to the outside door, "but they called right after lunch to confirm the date."

"Since he has to be in California next week, they decided to include a stop in Jerome while he's out west," Rachel explained quietly. She was the only one of the group who didn't look excited. In fact, she seemed dazed.

Who was "he"? Matthew wondered. As he walked forward, the group became aware of the new arrivals. Bonnie spun around. "Matthew, you'll never guess what's happened."

"We're going to have a visitor," he said calmly. That much he'd already figured out.

Darlene's grin was sly. "But not just any visitor."

"It's a once-in-a-lifetime occasion." That staunch pronouncement came from Ann.

"It's big," Bonnie declared, stretching her arms out wide.

"The President?" Matthew asked dryly.

"The Prince of Wales?" Jack tossed in from behind.

"Bigger than *that*," Bonnie said smugly. "It's—"

Diana broke in. "The drop-dead-handsome cover model—"

"Dirk Dahlstrom!" Dolores finished in a rush.

Over Bonnie's shoulder, Rachel's gaze locked with Matthew's.

"Rachel won an evening with Dirk Dahlstrom," Bonnie summed up, "and it's going to be *this Saturday night. That's BIG!*"

7

ON FRIDAY AFTERNOON, Rachel stood before a tall, three-way mirror in a dressing room at one of Flagstaff Mall's poshest clothing stores. She was there under protest, but she was there.

Her fate had been sealed that morning, she remembered, when she'd stated her intention to wear her old, reliable black cocktail dress on Saturday evening.

Bonnie had been aghast. "It's not good enough," she'd proclaimed, setting her hands on her hips.

"Why not?"

"It's...tired."

"I thought it was chic."

"It was chic five years ago, Rachel. Now it's tired. Besides, you have to wear something devastating. Dirk Dahlstrom must be used to being surrounded by gorgeous women."

Rachel had chuckled ruefully. "Well, he won't be with gorgeous tomorrow night," she'd said, referring to herself.

"He *could* be with gorgeous, if you'd make an effort."

"It's too late for plastic surgery, Bonnie."

Bonnie had blithely ignored the sarcasm. "It's not too late to find the most flattering creation you can and put yourself in it. In fact, it's exactly the time to get out of those T-shirts and jeans and scrap that tired dress. I was right about your winning the contest, and I'm right about this. Trust me."

Having developed a hearty new respect for her friend's "feelings," Rachel had trusted. Now, she studied the result.

The dress she wore was certainly a creation—what there was of it. Made of silvery satin, it resembled a full slip, with slender straps that displayed much of her back—and a lot of her front. Its short skirt showed a lengthy span of leg, as well.

"Holy moly!" That was Bonnie's judgment call after a prolonged, critical assessment. "It'll knock Dirk Dahlstrom on his beautiful buns. Guaranteed."

"I'm not sure it's me...or maybe it's too much of me."

"It's just enough, and you're on a fast track to gorgeous. All you need is an evening bag and some very high heels."

Rachel groaned. "Do you know how long it's been since my feet have worn very high *anything?*"

"They'll survive." Bonnie's eyes met Rachel's in the mirror. "This dress is perfect, and my grandmother has a beautiful lace shawl that will look great with it."

"Okay," she agreed resignedly. "It's an outlandish price for a piece of material, but I'll buy it. I want to get this over with and get back to the store. Remember, Matthew's handling it by himself for the first time."

"Relax. The man could handle a riot." Bonnie grinned a wicked grin. "But this little number you're wearing could probably knock *that* resourceful male on his rear end, too. It might even blow his circuits."

Rachel didn't respond. She was recalling the impressive sight of Matthew in tight Levi's and a denim shirt. A man who could look that good with four days' growth of dark beard was a threat to more than a woman's thought processes. She'd be wise to finish her shopping and forget him...if she could.

She soon found that she couldn't.

How did he feel about her impending date with Dirk Dahlstrom? she wondered as she chose a small silver evening bag. So far, the inscrutable Mr. Kent had given no clue as to his reaction. But he'd watched her intently, both yesterday and this morning before she'd left, as if he were waiting for something.

For what? she asked herself, taking her first steps on thin-strapped, high-high-heeled silver sandals. *Probably for you to fall at his feet and beg him to make love to you, Rach.* And her resolve to keep him at a distance was teetering, she had to admit. The time he'd been away had accomplished nothing, except to put him in her dreams— her wildest dreams.

Making love with Matthew Kent would be like falling off the mountain. She was sure of that. If it happened—if she let it happen—she might never recover.

BONNIE DROPPED Rachel at the store late that afternoon. As she walked in with her packages, the first thing she saw was a petite brunette with masterfully cut short hair standing at the counter. The second thing she saw was Matthew's smile, directed at the lovely, stylish woman. The third thing she saw was red. Which was ridiculous, she told herself, moving toward them. If Matthew chose to smile at anyone, that was his business.

Then her own forced smile turned genuine when she learned the visitor was Cynthia Renault. Rachel and the efficient, thirtyish, public-relations rep had spoken twice on the phone.

"I'm very pleased to meet you, Rachel," Cynthia said warmly. "I came a day early to finalize arrangements for Dirk's visit tomorrow, along with appearances he'll be making in Phoenix on Sunday. I wanted to check with you, however, before I made dinner reservations. How does L'Auberge in Sedona sound?"

Although she'd never been there, Rachel knew L'Auberge was one of the top-rated restaurants in Arizona. "It sounds wonderful," she said truthfully.

"I'd planned on making the reservation for two," Cynthia continued, smoothing a small hand over the jacket of her yellow linen suit, "but since Mr. Kent will be joining you—"

"Joining us?" Rachel aimed a sharp stare at Matthew.

He had that inscrutable look again. "You won the contest as a bookstore owner, didn't you?"

"Uh-huh," she agreed cautiously.

"Well, I believe I could be considered the joint owner, even though it's not official yet."

"And since Mr. Kent is going," Cynthia added as though there were no question, "I thought perhaps it would be appropriate if I included myself and made it a foursome."

Rachel totally ignored that last comment; her gaze was still riveted on Matthew. She couldn't believe it.

"You want to go on a date with Dirk Dahlstrom?"

HE DIDN'T WANT to go. *Hell,* Matthew grumbled to himself as he walked through the back door of the store at seven o'clock on Saturday evening, *he'd give almost anything not to go.* And here he was…going. He didn't even have a fellow male around to grouse to about the things men did for women. Jack had retreated to his cabin on the other side of Mingus Mountain yesterday.

"It's time for me to get away by myself for a while," Jack had said, his expression uncharacteristically sober. "I need to think on some things, Matt, but I'll be back before the six weeks are up." Then his wily grin had appeared. "I'm sure you can deal with all the hoopla better than I could."

Matthew didn't want to deal with it, but he would. There was no way—*no* way—he'd let Rachel spend an evening alone with Mr. Cover Model. So he'd donned a gray suit, white shirt and red silk tie, polished his black wing tips to a high gloss, and prepared to confront the inevitable.

As he entered the store area, Matthew saw Bonnie standing near the display window. With her were the other women who'd been there Thursday when he'd heard the very unwelcome news. They were all dressed to the nines, waiting for Dahlstrom, of course. Where was Rachel?

The abrupt sound of high heels coming down the back hall gave him his answer; he turned in response. Then she appeared and he heard nothing, was aware of nothing but the woman who approached and the sudden swell of desire.

He'd imagined Rachel's face flushed with passion. Now he saw her cheeks rosy—not with passion, but by design— and her glorious eyes accentuated in a crafty way that could make a man forget his name while it jabbed him with the undeniable knowledge that he was *male*. His muscles tightened as he felt the blow.

He'd tortured himself with images of how she would look without her usual practical clothing. Now he knew. God, did he know. Silky skin and knockout legs and an elegant neck left bare by her sophisticated, upswept hairstyle.

He'd physically ached after midnight visions of her full, soft breasts. Now he saw them. Not totally, of course, but the fragment of satin shielding them was a futile barrier to his imagination, and if she was wearing any sort of bra, he'd eat a piece of the gazebo. Come to think of it, having something to clench between his teeth might take the edge off his frustration at the impossible yet obstinate urge to touch her…everywhere.

And, to top it all off, he couldn't even take simple masculine satisfaction in the vision he gazed at.

Because Dirk Dahlstrom, damn him, was about to see it, too.

For one insane second Matthew thought about snatching the lacy shawl Rachel held over one arm and wrapping her in it from neck to knees. Then the women crowded around her, exclaiming how wonderful she looked. He stepped back and remained silent. If Rachel wasn't certain of his sentiments after his flagrant perusal of her, there would be no doubt in her mind on that score before the evening was over, he vowed. He would do everything in his power to take her to bed. *Tonight.*

Suddenly the front door opened and quiet swept over the room as three people entered. The first, a middle-aged man carrying a variety of camera equipment, stepped off to the side. Matthew figured he was the only one who'd even noticed him. Cynthia Renault, her smile as bright as the sequins on her short red dress, was next. Then came the man they'd been waiting for.

Dirk Dahlstrom had the strong, chiseled features, the shoulder-length, dark blond hair and the sea-colored eyes of a mythical Nordic warrior. He appeared to be in his early thirties, and he was a big man—his thick neck, broad shoulders and muscular body clearly were evident despite his clothing. And, of course, he wore blue, Matthew thought, noting the Armani suit, silk shirt and striped tie, all in various shades of that color. The color of the North Sea would show him to best advantage.

Yes, Dahlstrom was impressive, Matthew had to concede, though he'd drown himself in the Verde River before he'd admit it to anyone else.

"Holy...mother...moly," Bonnie whispered.

That small sound pierced the wall of silence. Cynthia introduced Dahlstrom to Rachel, who in turn introduced the other women. He shook hands and gave each a wide smile, displaying a string of gleaming white teeth. Darlene jumped up to kiss his tanned cheek, then did a mock swoon. Dahlstrom caught her in his arms and laughed. Flashbulbs popped as pictures were taken.

Then it was Matthew's turn to meet the man of the hour; Cynthia made the introduction.

"Nice to meet you, Mr. Kent," he said, extending a large hand. The voice was deep, the accent Midwestern. He might have flown in from the East, but this was no native New Yorker.

Being taller than average, Matthew seldom had to look up at anyone, yet he had to tilt his head back slightly to meet the other man's eyes. That irritated the hell out of him. It was petty, he knew. It annoyed him anyway. "The pleasure's all mine, Dahlstrom," he said as they shook hands.

While his words were scrupulously courteous, they were tinged with an irony that didn't go unnoticed, judging by the eyebrow Dahlstrom lifted in response. "I'm sure it will be a night to remember, Kent."

Damn right, Matthew agreed inwardly. *As soon as I can get rid of you.*

Rachel watched from a short distance away as the two men exchanged civilities. At least things seemed civil on Dirk Dahlstrom's part, she reflected. The rigid set of Matthew's jaw, however, made him look just a bit *un*civilized. She sighed softly. That sight didn't bode well for the evening to come.

DESPITE RACHEL'S misgivings, dinner started well. The restaurant was elegant, the decor country French, the service impeccable. The photographer took numerous pictures and departed. Both men opted for steaks; Rachel and Cynthia chose duck. They all had champagne. There were lots of smiles. Even Matthew bared his teeth now and then, Rachel noted. Cordiality reigned.

For a while.

Dirk, as he'd insisted Rachel call him, described how novel covers were produced, from the initial layout plans to the final versions on bookshelves. She asked questions about his part in the process. It was interesting. To Rachel.

"Must be hard work, Dahlstrom," Matthew said dryly as he sliced off a piece of steak.

She felt a sudden urge to kick him under the table.

Dirk shot him a knowing look. "I've worked harder. Growing up on a farm in Minnesota put more than a few calluses on my hands. Then I worked for a roofing company to earn enough money to get through college. Must have pounded in thousands of nails—though it seemed like a million at the time." He took a sip of champagne. "But the most challenging job I ever had was teaching Phys. Ed. to a bunch of teenage boys who were sure they knew more than I did." He chuckled. "*That* was hard work."

"Hmmm," was Matthew's sole comment. For a second. "And you gave all that up for fame and fortune?"

Now Rachel wanted to spear his hand with her fork.

"Actually I still spend some time at an inner-city high school in New York. We're building a new gym—"

"Dirk donated the funds," Cynthia tossed in.

"—in an effort to get the kids off the streets. And I may go back to teaching full-time someday."

"Hmmm." Matthew curled his fingers around the long stem of his glass. He opened his mouth. And clamped it shut with an audible gnashing of teeth when a high heel stomped down fiercely on his toes. A wince crossed his face, followed swiftly by a glare at Rachel. But it shut him up. For a while.

After dinner, they went dancing at one of Sedona's night-spots.

Dirk held Rachel in his arms. "Why do I get the impression Kent's aiming daggers at my back?" he asked with a grin, as they moved together to a lazy beat.

Rachel directed a glance past his wide shoulder to a small table and met Matthew's steely gaze over the top of Cynthia's head. She looked away. "Just ignore him," she advised.

"I'm trying. I have to admit it helps to have a lovely woman in my arms."

She was touched by his consideration. He was being charming, but it wasn't really necessary. "The only truly lovely woman in this group is sitting at the table."

He shook his head decisively. "You're wrong, Rachel."

Pulling back to look into those sea-blue eyes, she could almost believe that. Almost. "Thank you, Dirk."

"And you still don't quite accept it," he continued, as if he'd read her thoughts. "Even when your business partner is practically foaming at the mouth because I'm holding you." He lifted a brow. "Or *is* it just business?"

She sighed. "It has been." *Mostly.* "I'm not sure what it's going to be."

"He's probably a good man under that cynical exterior. Don't give him too much hell after the evening's over."

"Just a little," Rachel promised with mock gravity.

Dirk spun her around in a practiced turn. "But I'm not ready to let you go yet. We've got a lot more dancing to do, and then maybe a moonlight stroll by Oak Creek?"

"Only if I can take my shoes off. My feet aren't up to much more in these heels."

They smiled at each other...and became friends.

IN THE EARLY HOURS of the morning, they dropped Cynthia off at the Sedona resort where she and Dirk were staying, but he insisted on escorting his date home. So the three of them rode in the back of a long black limo, headed for Jerome.

Matthew sat across from the other two passengers. It was nearly over, he told himself, although he was no longer certain how the night would end. He had some fences to mend with Rachel. That was evident by the way she ignored him, giving all her attention to the man at her side as they chatted easily.

The most damnable thing about the whole evening was that Dirk Dahlstrom had turned out to be a nice guy, thought Matthew. He could almost have liked him, if the man in question hadn't been holding Rachel's shoes in the palm of one large hand. For some reason that possession seemed much too intimate.

He didn't want any man to hold Rachel—or even her shoes.

Except himself.

After what seemed like forever, at least to Matthew, the limo arrived at the store. It had scarcely come to a stop when he seized the silver sandals with a lightning-quick move and got out.

Dahlstrom looked down at his suddenly empty hand, then eyed Matthew with clear amusement. "I'd like a moment alone with my date, if you don't mind. You can keep the shoes. If the sidewalk's too cold, I can carry Rachel to the door."

"It's summer," he shot back. "She can walk."

"Speaking of walking," Rachel said calmly, "don't you have a dog that needs to be walked?"

He did. It would give him an excuse to return. He swung the door shut and heard a low, male chuckle before it closed. That made his temper rise, but he kept it in check. Barely.

Three minutes later he was back, Hodgepodge in tow. The limo was still parked by the curb, the door still closed. Through tinted glass Matthew could vaguely see its rear-seat occupants. They were talking, smiling at each other. "Come on, mutt," he said grimly, striding toward a small grassy area nearby. "This is going to be one of the shortest walks on record, so do your duty—fast."

Hodgepodge did. They returned and found the limo still parked there. Enough was enough, Matthew decided. He rapped sharply on the window.

The door opened and Dahlstrom got out, a wry grin curving his lips. He reached back through the opening to help Rachel. Matthew's hands fisted tightly at his sides. If she looked just-kissed, he decided he'd give serious consideration to kicking her escort in the butt. She didn't, he saw seconds later in the moonlight. The deep breath he took eased some of his tension.

After goodbyes were said, Dahlstrom reentered the car, glancing back to level a man-to-man look at Matthew. "Take care of her, Kent. She deserves the best." Then he shut the door and the limo pulled away.

Rachel watched its red taillights disappear down the street. Matthew watched Rachel. "If your feet are cold, I can carry you," he offered. It was an attempt at an apology. He saw her recognition of that fact when she turned to face him.

"I'm fine," she said, just two quiet words that conveyed nothing of her feelings. Then she started for the door.

He followed her, Hodgepodge at his side. They walked through the store and up the back stairs in a silence so alive he could almost feel it pulsing. When they reached the second-floor landing, he couldn't just let her go, so he grasped a shawl-covered arm to halt her as she turned toward the stairs to the third floor. "I'd like to talk to you. May I come up after I get the dog settled?"

One second lengthened to five before she said, "All right. I'll...pour you a brandy."

It was more than he deserved, he knew. And infinitely less than he wanted. Yet even if that was all he could have, he'd damn well take it. "I'll be there in a few minutes."

RACHEL STUDIED the amber-colored liquid she'd just poured into a small snifter and leaned a hip against the counter. She didn't want to—couldn't—sit down yet, although her feet were protesting her vertical position. She felt too edgy to sit. Besides, she told herself, she'd only have to get up again when Matthew came. He'd be there soon. That was why her nerves were bouncing off the kitchen walls.

Sighing softly, she closed her eyes. It was a mistake—a big one—because a vivid memory of something she'd succeeded in blocking from her mind for several hours stormed in: Matthew Kent's hard face, taut with desire as he'd watched her enter the store much earlier that evening. In that spellbinding moment, she'd heard his thoughts as clearly as if he'd roared them. He would make an effort to take her to bed. *Tonight.*

Did she want him to make love to her? Yes. She couldn't deceive herself about that. Even if she tried, her body wouldn't let her get away with it.

Was she going to let him make love to her? She honestly didn't know. All she was certain of was that it would be her decision now. Matthew had already made his. If she agreed to become his lover, he wouldn't hesitate. He was a man of action.

So, it was up to her, she concluded as a quiet knock sounded.

Seconds later Rachel faced Matthew through the opened doorway. He'd removed his suit coat and tie, and undone the top buttons of his white shirt. His shirtsleeves were rolled up to the elbows. He'd returned to his "casual" attire. She nearly smiled at that, but those nerves wouldn't quite let her.

"Come in," she invited with a calmness she was far from feeling. She handed him the glass of brandy she'd brought with her and closed the door. "Let's go into the living room."

Matthew followed as she walked down the hall. She sat on one end of the long, wine-colored chintz sofa; he took the other and stretched his legs out in front of him. Holding the snifter in the palm of one hand, he turned his head to look at her. "I forgot to bring your shoes."

They were going to talk about shoes? Well, she was ready to discuss anything to break the quiet. Anything but the most vital thing: the crossroads they had come to, the path *she* had to choose. "That's okay. I won't be needing them for a while."

He sipped his drink. "Come to think of it, I'm not sure I should give them back."

Puzzled, she frowned. "Why?"

"You'll probably slip into them and go off for another evening with some devastating Mr. Whoever, and I'll wind up imitating a jackass and getting my toes stomped on."

It was such a candid account of the night's events that she had to grin. He might be supremely self-assured and orderly to a fault, but he wasn't above joking about himself. His self-deprecating admission had proved that. She relaxed a little, just enough to be able to tease him a bit. "Those high heels came in handy, I have to admit. Maybe I should market my own special design."

His mouth curved widely. As always when he smiled— really smiled—she felt the powerful pull. "The stop-the-man-with-a-stomp model?" he ventured wryly.

She pretended to deliberate for a moment. "It might have possibilities, especially with a video to demonstrate the technique. Are you willing to volunteer?"

He lifted an eyebrow. "Hell, no. My toes haven't recovered from your last demonstration."

She could sympathize. Wiggling her own toes, she winced.

Instantly his expression turned serious. "What's the matter? Did you hurt yourself?"

"Nothing terminal," she assured him solemnly. "The only thing hurting is my feet. They're killing me."

His sharp bark of laughter told her she'd surprised him. "Serves you right for all that gadding about, but I'll take pity on you anyway." Before she could guess his intent, he set his glass aside and bent down to grasp her nylon-clad ankles. One fluid movement later, her feet were in his lap, resting on hard thighs. "You're not the only one who can give massages, you know."

She opened her mouth to say...something...and heard a small, blissful moan emerge from her throat as his thumbs deftly rotated against the ball of one foot, and then went on to rub her toes, arch, heel and ankle. "Where did you learn to do that?" she asked in little more than a whisper as he started the process all over again on her other foot.

"In the Far East," he replied, his voice low. "They have a great respect for the art of massage. The foot, in particular, contains pleasure points that affect the entire body."

She could well believe that, because she was undeniably being pleasured by his skillful touch. And it went far beyond her feet. Oh, Lord, yes. It swept over her, burrowed into her, even in—*especially in*—the most personal parts of her. In some magical way, he was stroking her... everywhere.

If you're going to stop this—stop him—it has to be soon, an inner voice told her. But she could wait a moment to decide, another part of her rationalized. Just a moment...

Matthew watched Rachel's face intently in the soft light cast by the lamp next to the sofa. Her eyes were closed, her mouth open slightly, her breath coming fast enough to tell him he was pleasing her. Exciting her. *Arousing her.* That knowledge speeded his own breath as he slid his gaze downward until it reached her legs. Knockout legs. He slipped his palms beneath them, and that small movement sent silvery satin rising half an inch up her well-rounded thighs.

Instantly his maleness rose to strain against his zipper; he had to crush his lips together to hold back a groan. He continued to rub her soft calves, feeling tiny, tight muscles loosen under his touch. He'd seen his fair share of female flesh, and yet had always retained command over his body until he'd willingly abandoned it to bring his partner and himself to fulfillment.

No, it wasn't merely the sight of womanly flesh that was testing the limits of his restraint.

It was *this* woman's flesh.

"Rachel, look at me," he ordered in a husky rasp. It was a moment before her eyes fluttered open, then slowly widened as they fixed on his face. They stared at each other as he continued to stroke her legs. "I want you as badly as I've ever wanted anything." It was a stark statement. "But I can't give you hearts and flowers and promises of a happy ending. What I can give you is physical pleasure and fidelity for as long as it lasts between us." His hands stilled. "I want you," he repeated, "but I won't make love to you unless you're willing to settle for what I can offer."

He's offering an affair, thought Rachel. It didn't surprise her. She knew he didn't believe in romance. Or love. He might never be able to make a real commitment to a woman—even one he wanted badly. If he'd spoken flowery phrases in an attempt to take her to bed, she would have scorned them as patently false. Then she could have flatly refused him. But he'd been forthright, and she wasn't surprised or offended by his candor.

No, the only thing that surprised her was the way *she* felt, because she was feeling…reckless. She, a woman who had always considered the future, who valued loving emotions and lifelong commitments, suddenly longed to live for the moment and make love with a man who didn't believe in love.

Reason would return, she knew, accompanied perhaps by regret. Tomorrow. "I want you, too, and I'll take whatever you can give…but I may not be able to give *you* pleasure. It's been a long time for me, and—"

Speech died as he spread her legs, launched himself forward and came down on her with such lightning quickness it rendered her mute. He rested his weight on his elbows, holding his chest inches above her breasts. His swift action had driven her dress up far past modesty, and his lower body was now pressed intimately to hers—his narrow hips wedged between her thighs, his rigid arousal hard against her very private softness.

"Don't for one minute think you can't please me," he said in a virtual growl. "You've been driving me crazy for weeks, witchy woman. I'm going to show you exactly how much."

Then he lowered his mouth to capture hers, thrusting his tongue inside without a second's hesitation. The kiss was deeper, hotter, longer, hungrier than any they had shared before. By the time it ended, they were both gasping for breath.

Rachel was still forcing air in and out of her lungs as Matthew trailed his lips down her throat, past her collarbone, to the bodice of her dress. And he didn't stop there. One slender strap slid off her shoulder and down her arm as he nudged the slippery satin aside and continued on his way, baring her breast in the process, until he reached her nipple.

Again, he didn't hesitate for an instant. He took the pebbled tip into his mouth and sucked with a seductive rhythm that soon had her tunneling her fingers in his silky hair to hold him to her—and to hold on to *something* as she reeled from the overwhelmingly rapid onslaught on her body and senses.

This would be no leisurely, gentle loving, she realized. Nothing at all like the tender moments of sexual union she'd known in the past. No, making love with Matthew Kent, at least this time, would be basic. Elemental. And perhaps too fast for her to match his pace. Would he give her time to…?

That question and what little reasoning processes she had left went up in smoke when he suddenly lifted his head, heating her from the inside out with a burning stare as he put one large hand, palm up, between her legs.

"You're ready for me," he said with satisfaction. "I can feel the wetness even through your panty hose. It's time to get rid of them." With that, he rose up, slipped both hands beneath her dress, and drew her panty hose and lace panties down her legs and over her feet in one long movement. Immediately he grasped her waist and lifted her, then sat back against the cushions and lowered her in such a fashion that she wound up straddling his thighs. His hands had scarcely released her when he pulled a small foil packet from his pocket and reached for his zipper.

"Let's go to bed," Rachel said hastily, abruptly aware that he intended to take her right then and there, on the sofa, with the light shining down on them, right in the middle of her living room!

"I'll never make it to the bed." It was a blunt, guttural declaration punctuated by the harsh sound of the zipper's plunge.

He wants me that much, she thought, closing her eyes because she didn't know where to look while he donned protection. A lingering doubt that she could please him disappeared, although events might be proceeding too quickly for her.

Only a few seconds passed before he reached under her

dress, put his hands on her bare hips and brought her closer. "Rachel, look at me." She looked…and found him watching her intently. "I want to see those green eyes when I—" He started to enter her. "God, you feel so warm. So tight. So damn good."

No, he was the one who felt good. He'd told her she was ready, but she hadn't quite believed it—couldn't believe now how easily her body accepted him, as if it had been waiting for this man. He deepened their joining and started to thrust with long, slow, sinuous strokes. Clutching his broad shoulders, she began to move in tandem with him and received a throaty male groan in reward. And that good feeling swiftly turned to…*wonderful.*

Their gazes were still locked when *marvelous* blossomed inside Rachel, supplanting wonderful. Then marvelous became *fabulous.* And fabulous was transformed into *fantastic.* Oh, Lord, it was the most fantastic sensation she'd ever experienced.

That was when the pain hit her.

It was a sudden sharp slash of longing that sliced through her and had her panting. Matthew had promised pleasure, but he hadn't mentioned the keen, raw ache his lovemaking was creating. It seemed foreign. Alien. Instinctively she tried to pull away, certain it would take her somewhere she had never been before.

Strong arms crushed her closer as he speeded his thrusts. "Don't fight it, Rachel. Give yourself up to it. I'll go with you. We'll let it take us both."

Then, without warning, it took her—*he* took her—past pain, past bliss, past everything remotely familiar to her, all the way to…rapture. Small yet mighty convulsions swept through her, culminating in a climax so total the whole world went blindingly white. She squeezed her eyes tight and cried out, "Matthew!"

Matthew allowed himself one last look at Rachel's face,

vibrant with passionate release and unmistakable awe at having achieved it. Then he closed his eyes and prepared to surrender. It was a testimony to sheer determination that he'd lasted as long as he had, he knew, because he'd been ready to explode from the moment he'd entered her. With one final, deep thrust, going as far as he could go, he erupted forcefully. Powerful spasms ripped through his body, and he heard his low shout pierce the stillness as the woman in his arms collapsed against him.

God, it felt so *right*.

Gradually Matthew returned to reality and was welcomed by the scent of a light, floral perfume mingled with the musky smell of sex. He inhaled that heady essence as he moved his mouth to whisper in a delicately shaped ear. "Have you come back yet?"

"Mmmm," was Rachel's only response. Her face remained nuzzled in the crook of his neck.

"How do you feel?"

She sighed softly. "My feet don't hurt anymore."

His chuckle was a gravelly rumble. "I'm glad all my efforts accomplished *something*." He brushed his fingers over the nape of her neck. "I can't believe that after all that, I still haven't seen your hair down." Gently he removed several small pins and laid them in a neat pile on the table next to the sofa. "Sit up and let me look at you."

Rachel slowly raised her head and straightened; her gaze was drowsy as Matthew arranged her long hair over her creamy shoulders. One dress strap remained where it had fallen to expose the top of a breast. She looked like a well-loved woman, he decided, and he had to have her again. Very, very soon. "I want to see your hair spread on a pillow. Are you ready to go to bed?"

She gave him a lazy smile. "Can you make it *now*?"

His sudden smile was frankly wicked. "I can do any

number of things *now*, and I plan on doing all of them. In fact, I'm going to do my best to make good on that reward voucher and give you the night of your wildest dreams.''

8

It wasn't a night for sleep. Again and again, Matthew took Rachel with him on a sensual journey. He asked what she wanted, demanded she tell him everything that would please her, and gave it to her without hesitation. When she ran out of suggestions, he came up with several inventive ones of his own. Between times, they dozed briefly and then continued on their journey, until both were exhausted.

Finally they slept.

Matthew woke sometime after the sun had risen; the long, pale shadows slanting across the bed through lace-curtained windows facing east told him it was still very early. Rachel was pressed to him, her lithe back against his chest, her soft bottom against his groin.

He had pleasured this woman as she had never been pleasured before. He was certain of that. And in the process he had found unparalleled pleasure in her.

Yawning contentedly, Matthew allowed his mind to drift for a moment, until he felt an abrupt sense of something that needed to be done. He had to walk the dog, but that could wait for a while, he decided, nudging closer to Rachel and feeling his maleness stir. He was also out of condoms, which meant a trip downstairs to replenish his supply. That couldn't wait much longer, given the way his body was responding even after hours of exertion that should have left him sated, yet clearly hadn't.

When would his hunger for her ease? he wondered as he made himself move away. *Not anytime soon,* something inside him answered with firm conviction. He rose, grabbed the floral-print sheet and dark green comforter bunched at the foot of the antique brass bed, and pulled them up to cover a sleeping Rachel. The spell she'd cast was too potent to weaken quickly, he mused. While it persisted, he'd enjoy to the utmost the pleasure she gave him. For now, however, he had to let her get some rest.

Dressing as quietly as possible, Matthew looked around the room he'd barely noticed the night before. Then, his only priority had been a bed—period—but he remembered a brief moment of surprise at the fact that Rachel occupied the back bedroom. He'd assumed she was using the front one, since it would be larger. Yet there was a compelling reason to choose this room, he thought, looking toward a tall window then through airy lace to see red-hued mountains in the distance. That view was even more spectacular than the one visible from the second floor. Buttoning his shirt, Matthew left the bedroom and his sleeping lover. He would be back. He knew he couldn't stay away.

"Woof."

"Shush, mutt. She's still asleep."

Those sounds reached Rachel as she drifted languidly toward consciousness. Her face remained snuggled in the pillow while the bedroom door was quietly shut and footsteps approached the bed. Suddenly a mournful whimpering started from the hall. The steps retreated, accompanied by Matthew's soft curse. Then the door was opened and swiftly closed. She could hear him talking on the other side, although his low words were indistinguishable.

A minute later he was back, shutting the door behind him. This time only the rustle of clothing and slow slide of a zipper broke the silence before he lifted the covers and got into bed.

"What was that all about?" she murmured groggily, her

eyes still closed. She wasn't quite ready to face the light of day or the reality of the night before.

"Sorry we woke you," he said, wrapping one sinewy arm around her waist from behind. Gently he rolled her over and settled her against him so that her head rested on a broad, bare shoulder. She realized the rest of him was bare, too, under their cocoon of bedcovers. "I had to explain some facts to my canine acquaintance, but he'll be quiet now."

"What did you tell him?"

"That he had to stay out of the bedroom and quit whining because every male's entitled to some privacy in his sex life."

Smiling wryly, Rachel felt crispy chest hair beneath her cheek. "And Hodgepodge understood completely?"

"Sure. He's got more brains than some people I've met."

She detected a hint of pride in that statement. "For a man who told me not too long ago that he didn't like dogs, you seem to have become rather fond of this particular one."

"The mutt's okay," Matthew allowed, "even if he does drool on me every now and then." He threaded the long fingers of one hand through her tousled hair. "Now if *you* wanted to drool over me..." He let that sentence trail off suggestively.

Her soft laugh abruptly transformed into a yawn. "I might be too tired to drool now."

"That's all right, a rain check will do. Since I took the mutt for a brisk walk over most of Jerome and followed it with a cold shower, my body may give me a break and let me get a little more rest myself."

She yawned again; she couldn't help it. "Thank goodness the store doesn't open until noon on Sunday."

"I'll second that." He brought her even closer and ran

a soothing hand up and down her spine. "Go to sleep, Rachel."

She did.

ALMOST TWO HOURS later Rachel was fixing breakfast. She wore her white terry-cloth robe; her hair hung damply down her back. Hodgepodge sat on the kitchen floor, overseeing her efforts as she removed crisp bacon from a sizzling skillet.

This time she'd been the one who'd left a sleeping Matthew in bed and risen to take a shower—although the water she'd used for her own had been very warm, bordering on hot, in an attempt to ease muscles that protested the night's activities.

It hadn't been the night of her wildest dreams.

It had been infinitely more, she thought, because she couldn't have dreamed about some of the things that had transpired. They'd been far beyond her experience and even past her ability to fantasize—certainly with herself in a leading role. And they'd definitely been wild. And sweet. And unforgettable.

Matthew Kent was a highly skilled and equally generous lover—that was one more fact she'd learned about him.

Any regrets, Rach? she silently asked herself.

"No, not a one," she immediately answered out loud, and meant it. It would have been unpardonably foolish of her to regret even a second of the whole, long night's wondrous events.

A low bark greeted her statement. She smiled down at the dog. "I guess you agree, sweetie. But then, you think the man I spent the night with walks on water, don't you?"

Hodgepodge panted enthusiastically.

Chuckling softly, Rachel pulled a white Formica bed tray from a cabinet. She unfolded its short wooden legs and placed it on the counter. Soon that tray held the meal she'd prepared: French toast with butter and maple syrup, bacon, a small glass of orange juice, and two mugs of coffee.

Rachel picked up the tray and crossed the hall. She'd left the bedroom door open a crack, so a slight nudge with one hip swung it ajar. She glanced back before pushing it closed and saw Hodgepodge sprawl peacefully on the hall carpet, apparently heeding Matthew's male-to-male chat. Her lips twitched in amusement as she turned toward the bed. But that grin quickly faded at the sight her gaze encountered.

At some point, Matthew had shrugged off the bedcovers. All of them. He was lying on his side, his back to the door, giving her a totally unrestricted rear view of a naked male body. Dark, sleep-mussed hair, corded neck, wide shoulders tapering to a trim waist, narrow hips, tight buttocks, well-muscled thighs and long, long legs. Although she'd seen him—all of him—the night before, the dim bedroom lighting had lessened the impact. Now, bright sunshine outlined every inch with blatant clarity.

As she moved forward, still giving that sight a pleasurable once-over, he suddenly shifted, turning toward her until he was stretched out flat on the bed.

But one very male part of him that had just come into view stood straight and tall.

Oh, Lord! Rachel jolted to a dead halt and nearly dropped the tray. Silverware clattered against a plate. Hastily she raised her gaze from Matthew's groin to his face and found his gray eyes slanting open to observe her. For an endless moment they stared at each other in the hushed silence.

He made no attempt to cover himself; he merely lifted an unabashed eyebrow. "Is that tray for me?" he asked, finally glancing away to look at her burden.

Is that arousal for me? she almost blurted out, catching herself in the nick of time as her brain kicked in.

"I...ah...remembered the reward voucher you won and decided to serve you breakfast in bed."

Smiling faintly, he sat up and stacked a pillow behind him, then reclined against the shiny brass headboard. "You'll have to come closer if I'm going to get fed," he pointed out reasonably.

He wouldn't even pull the sheet over him! She hadn't blushed since she was a teenager, but she felt her cheeks heating. "Can you eat in that...ah...condition?" she murmured, walking ahead with her gaze fixed firmly on his face.

His smile grew...and grew. "I'll certainly try...Rosie." This time his use of that nickname was a clear reference to her blush. She studiously ignored it and kept going until she reached his side. There, he took the tray from her and lowered it over his lap. "You can look down now. I'm decent again."

Decent? Technically. The bed tray covered a strategic area, she saw with a rapid glance, but they both knew what was under it. That knowledge seemed as intimate as anything they had shared the night before. "You'd better eat before it gets cold," she said as casually as she could manage. Then she moved to the other side of the bed, propped a pillow against the headboard and sat back with her robe securely tucked around her.

"All this food is for me?" he asked with equal nonchalance as he handed her one of the mugs.

"Uh-huh. I've already eaten," she told him before taking a welcome sip of hot coffee. Although that wasn't the whole truth, it was close enough. She'd nibbled, but her stomach was too full of butterflies to consume an entire meal.

Obviously having no problem with *his* digestive system, Matthew drank the orange juice in one long swallow and took a large bite of French toast. He caught an errant drop of syrup with the tip of his tongue. "This is terrific."

"I can do the basics well enough." One corner of her mouth edged upward. "Of course, I don't have *flair*."

He met the teasing look she tossed his way. "You have other attributes," he assured her. His eyes swept over her. "Even hidden by that old robe—which is sexy as hell when *you're* in it, by the way—I can visualize some of them...vividly."

Her heart skipped a beat, but she had no reply. Instead, she silently stared ahead and soon heard him munching on a strip of bacon. It was time for a switch in subject, she decided. "What do they usually have for breakfast in the Orient?"

Matthew recognized the intent behind that question, but he was willing to have the conversation diverted...for a while. It might even help to assuage his "condition," he thought. At least until he could remedy it in a far more effective way. So he spent the next few minutes detailing the eating customs he'd noted in the various Far Eastern countries he'd visited while he finished his breakfast. "I've enjoyed the time I've spent there and the people I've met," he said truthfully, "although I won't be visiting nearly as often in the future."

"I remember reading that you had sold Kent Enterprises' interests in that part of the world."

He nodded. "I know rumors are rife that I'm downsizing the company—and it's true." Those last words were uttered before he'd even considered them. He was surprised at the ease with which they'd been issued. When it came to business, he was an extremely discreet man. Other than a long discussion with Lou Arlington and a few other key employees before he'd put his plan into action, this was the only time he'd voiced his goals. Yet, for some reason, it felt natural to discuss the matter now.

"As you probably know," he continued, "Kent Enterprises is basically an investment firm holding a minority interest in many large corporations. I've begun the process of divesting most of those interests in order to concentrate on a smaller entrepreneurial group of businesses based here in the western United States—ones that need extensive capital backing to expand into new markets."

Rachel set her mug down on the oak nightstand. "Sounds interesting. Do you mind if I ask why?"

Why? He didn't totally understand all the nuances of his motives himself. He was certainly going against everything his father had envisioned for the company. "I like the challenge of breaking new ground," he said as he lifted his gaze to the ceiling. He was thinking out loud as much as speaking to the woman beside him. "It would be a chance to contribute to the real birth of something, rather than just earning a part of the profits on the investment. It would also mean a lot less traveling than I've had to do in the past."

"And perhaps a little more time for yourself?"

Matthew drew his brows together in a slight frown. "For myself?" Had that been part of his motivation? he wondered. It was the first time he'd consciously considered that aspect of it, but he'd certainly have more free time.

"Like a weekend off once in a while, and maybe not putting in more than say, twelve hours a day on the job?" Rachel clarified with a hefty dose of irony. "And every so often a—dare I mention the word?—*vacation.*"

Lowering his eyes, he speared her with a mock-stern stare. "Are you by any chance having a laugh at my expense?"

Her eyes widened innocently. "I wouldn't dream of it. But, just for the record, have you had any headaches lately?"

"Because I'm on vacation?" he hedged, knowing she'd be smugly pleased with the truth.

"Exactly."

"No, I haven't had any headaches," he admitted, dropping his voice to an intimate level. "I've had too many aches in another part of my anatomy to notice any pain in my head." With that, he lifted the tray off his lap and set it on the floor next to the bed. Turning back swiftly, he was gratified to see that her green eyes had widened even further.

"I remember something about a 'dessert of my choice' listed on that reward voucher," he said huskily as he shot one strong arm out and wrapped it around Rachel's waist. Inexorably, he pulled her closer. "Come here, witchy woman. *You're dessert.*"

Then Matthew proceeded to relish his treat.

It turned out to be the best dessert he'd ever had.

"ARE YOU the fie-nan-ee-al goo-roo?" Darcy Gallico asked with a child's blunt directness. Bonnie's daughter was spending a Saturday afternoon at the store. It was late in the day, the first day of the Labor Day weekend. While Rachel and Bonnie waited on last-minute customers and prepared for the store's imminent closing, Darcy had discovered Matthew in the office. They'd been introduced earlier, but the dark-haired, dark-eyed girl hadn't had a chance to conduct a serious interrogation—until now. "Maybe I didn't get it right," she added, clearly noting Matthew's puzzled look. "It was something my mommy said."

"I think she meant financial guru," he explained calmly as realization dawned, "and I guess I'm him."

"What does a goo-roo do?"

Matthew settled back in the desk chair. "He plays with numbers." It was as good a description as any, he figured.

"Like on Sesame Street?"

Nodding matter-of-factly, Matthew bit back the urge to grin. He didn't want this little person who stood before him wearing a bright pink cotton sundress to think he was making fun of her, because he wasn't. He didn't much care for adults who dealt with children's curiosity in that manner, or those who condescended to them. He'd had enough of that himself when he was a young boy and his father had trotted him out at social functions to be shown off as the heir to the Kent legacy.

Not that he knew all that much about kids, he had to concede. He hadn't been around them very much. In fact, if he had ever actually had a true discussion with a child since he'd become an adult, he couldn't remember it. He found this one's frankness refreshing. He had a hunch a person would always know where they stood with Darcy Gallico.

"Do you play with the computer, too?" she asked with a glance at the inventory program displayed on the monitor. At his nod, she said, "I'll be in first grade when school starts this year." It was a proud declaration. "I'm going to learn about computers and take flying lessons and become an astronaut. This is my very favorite ball—" she lifted one hand to display a small ball decorated to resemble a globe "—because it looks like the world. I'll be looking down at the world someday."

And she just might, thought Matthew. She appeared to be a very determined six-year-old. "I think that's an admirable ambition."

"I'll wave at you when I'm up there," she said earnestly. "I promise."

For some reason those words touched him in a place he hadn't realized existed inside himself until that moment. "I promise to wave back." It was the only reply he could come up with, but it seemed acceptable, judging by her beatific smile.

Her eager dark eyes met his. "Could you teach me a little about computers—please—so I can get up there quicker?"

He started to say no and found he couldn't; he'd been beguiled by a gap-toothed smile. Who would have believed it? Certainly none of his business associates. Sighing, he gave himself up to his fate. "Okay, we'll have a quick lesson."

"Yippee!" Darcy jumped up and down. "Goo-roos are great!"

Matthew had to laugh.

Several yards away in the store area, Bonnie stood next to the cash register. As she bagged a purchase, she turned her head toward the hall doorway. "Sounds like they're having a pretty good time back there. I hope Darcy's not being too much of a bother."

Rachel completed a transaction with the last customer in line. "Matthew can handle it," she said, although she wasn't as confident as she tried to sound. She had no idea how much patience Matthew would have when dealing with a young child.

Bonnie locked the door behind the departing customer and switched the sign in the window to Closed. "Speaking of handling," she said casually as she returned to the register, "the orderly man seems to be handling *you* rather well."

"What makes you say that?" Rachel asked cautiously.

"It would be downright impossible not to realize that something's going on, Rachel. The glances you two have been aiming at each other for the past few days would melt concrete. Now, do you want to talk about it, or should I keep my mouth shut and pretend I've developed major problems with my vision?"

Leaning forward, Rachel folded her arms on the glass counter. "I guess, since the jig's up, we might as well discuss it.'' She hesitated, then decided to just come out and say it. ''Matthew and I have become lovers.''

Bonnie slapped one hand down on the counter. ''I knew it! And I'll bet it happened last Saturday.'' Not waiting for a response, she forged on. ''I saw how he looked at you when you made your entrance in that dress. It was a wonder the building didn't catch fire. But he's been looking at you the same way all this week, even though you're back in T-shirts and jeans. I'd say he's got it bad, and so do you, if the way you've been returning those looks is any indication.''

Rachel tucked a wayward lock of hair behind her ear. She'd been wearing it down because Matthew had asked her to; he liked it that way. She'd also given in to his request to be with her, in her bed, all night, every night. Of course, she wanted that as much as he did. What disturbed her was the burgeoning need to have him there—a need that went beyond the purely physical.

Still, she had no regrets, absolutely none, about making love with Matthew Kent. But she had doubts, plenty of them, concerning the future. In two weeks he would receive his inheritance. What would happen when—

''I can see your circuits have been blown again,'' Bonnie remarked fatalistically, ''and maybe your ability to focus, too. You're staring straight through me.''

Rachel fixed her attention staunchly on her friend. ''I'm fine. I just didn't get much sleep last night.'' Instantly she could have rammed her knuckles down her too-candid throat for making that truthful statement.

Bonnie's delicately arched brows shot up. ''Well, it seems the man has stamina to add to his list of virtues.''

Eyes narrowing, Rachel launched a warning glance.

''All right, I'll drop that fascinating topic,'' Bonnie said with an unrepentant grin. ''I won't even mention how glowing, how…satisfied you look.'' Then her expression sobered. "I hope you'll go on looking that way, that you'll be happy. I don't know how serious this thing is on his part, but for you—"

Gently Rachel broke in. "It's an affair, for as long as it lasts. Matthew and I both know that." And she wasn't going to delude herself or anyone else about it.

Bonnie frowned. "Is that enough for you?"

"Yes," she replied calmly. It would have to be. She'd make it enough, for however long she spent her nights in his arms.

Bonnie studied her for a long moment. "I'm not sure it's going to turn out that way, Rachel, but this time I *will* keep my mouth shut if I have to wire it closed."

A teasing gleam entered Rachel's eyes. "Shall I call your husband to tell him the good news?"

Bonnie smiled widely. "He wouldn't believe it." She began to inspect the day's receipts. "Wow, look at all these sales. It's going to take some time to close tonight."

"I'll go check on Darcy while you get started," Rachel said, walking toward the back hall.

"Good idea. Check on Matthew, too," Bonnie threw in slyly. "The poor man might not have the strength to deal with a six-year-old much longer after all his efforts last night."

Rachel spun around and raised a mock-threatening fist.

Lifting her hands in a gesture of surrender, Bonnie said, "Okay, okay. Go!"

She went. As she approached the office, she heard Matthew's low voice issuing a patient explanation. "Then you press that key. Yes, just like that." Immediately the printer hummed to life. "Excellent. Your page will come out in a second and we can see how it looks."

Rachel stopped in the doorway and viewed the sight before her. Darcy was kneeling in the swivel chair. Her small hands brushed reverently over the sides of the computer keyboard, as though it were a magical device. Matthew leaned against the desk, arms crossed over his chest. He seemed totally at ease. Hodgepodge nudged Darcy's ball across the floor with his black nose.

A moment later Matthew plucked the sheet from the laser printer and handed it to Darcy. "You did a great job," he told her very seriously. "You should be proud."

"Holy moly!" Darcy exclaimed with unmistakable awe, staring down at the paper.

Rachel couldn't hold back a soft laugh at that perfect imitation of Bonnie. Immediately three heads, two human and one canine, turned her way.

Scrambling out of the chair, Darcy began to talk a mile a minute. "Aunt Rachel, you'll never guess what. I typed out my ABCs, and then we copied them, over and over, and made some bigger and some smaller. And now—" she proudly displayed her accomplishment "—I have a whole sheet of them!"

"That's wonderful, honey," Rachel said, smiling.

Darcy turned back to Matthew. "Can we do another one, please? This time with all the numbers I can count up to."

Rachel thought about intervening, but the it's-all-right glance Matthew sent her way kept her quiet. "Okay, one more," he told Darcy, who was gazing hopefully up at him, "after I load the printer. That red light means it's out of paper. You'll have to be patient." He retrieved a pack of paper from the cupboard and began to load it.

Darcy nodded. "I know what *patient* means. When Mommy and Daddy close their bedroom door sometimes in the afternoon, Grandma says I have to be patient and leave them alone for a while. So I play with my toys until the door opens. Mommy always comes out smiling, but sometimes Daddy gets awful tired and has to take a nap."

Rachel heard Matthew's deep, swiftly smothered chuckle. Somehow she managed to retain a suitably composed expression. ''Well, it's good that you know how to be...patient.''

''I know what *secret* means, too,'' Darcy rushed on. ''It's like the place under the rug in the living room where Mommy and Daddy keep the extra money for a rainy—''

''We're ready,'' Matthew broke in smoothly. He slanted a decidedly wicked look of amusement at Rachel, then gazed down. ''One more page, future astronaut. Then I have to walk the dog.''

''Can I help you walk the dog?''

''All right, if your mother agrees,'' Matthew said, smiling. ''But while we walk, we're going to have a talk about the word *secret*. I don't think you completely understand the concept.''

''Okay,'' Darcy said amenably, climbing back in the chair. ''What's a *concept?*''

Rachel had to bite her tongue to keep from laughing. Perhaps the self-assured man had finally met his match.

''WHO'S THAT MAN Matthew's talking with?'' Bonnie asked.

Rachel finished counting the last of the dollar bills in her hand and glanced out the front window. Matthew and Darcy had returned from their walk. They were across the street, in front of the large building now in its last stages of renovation. Its doors and windows had been replaced, and the dark, dingy brick had been sandblasted to a honey-beige, just-like-new condition. There was a silver, top-of-the-line Cadillac parked at the curb.

Darcy stood on the sidewalk, bouncing her ball. Seated beside her, Hodgepodge watched it go up and down, following its movements as though he were viewing a vertical tennis match. A few feet away, Matthew spoke with a man, probably in his forties judging by the white streaks in his brown hair, who was leaning against the hood of the luxury car. Everything about the man—his demeanor, his stylish raw-silk tan suit, his vehicle—positively shouted *Wealth!*

"I don't know who he is," Rachel replied. "I don't think I've ever seen him before."

Still gazing out the window, Bonnie sighed. After a long moment, she spoke again. "I hate to say this—I *really* hate to say this—but I've got a feeling about that conversation, and it's not good." She turned to look at Rachel, her face somber. "In fact, it's pretty bad."

Rachel wanted to shrug aside her friend's "bad feeling," but couldn't. She recalled another feeling that had been all too prophetic. Suddenly a chill of foreboding crawled down her spine. "How bad?"

"Bad enough to make me hope I never feel it again."

Rachel mulled those words over as she and an uncharacteristically subdued Bonnie silently continued their task. *Bad enough to make me hope I never feel it again.* What in the world could be so ominous about a mere chance conversation? Or had it been merely chance? she asked herself as a very unwelcome possibility entered her mind. She didn't want to consider it, yet she had to. Because it *was* possible.

While the man in question was a stranger to her, he might not be a stranger to Matthew. That in itself wasn't so unusual. His circle of acquaintances had to be wide, including people of wealth. But what if the man was somehow connected with Kent Enterprises? That would be ominous indeed, since any contact between the two men would be a direct breach of the terms of Ava's will.

Everything about Matthew's manner—his easy stance as he spoke with the other man, the way his hands rested casually in the pockets of his gray wool pants, his cordial yet not overly friendly expression—told her she was letting her imagination override her common sense. Even more compelling was an inner conviction that the man who had become her lover was a person of integrity. Ava had believed that; Rachel believed it, too. If he decided for some reason not to comply with the will's provisions, he wouldn't do it in an underhanded fashion.

But his business is supremely important to him, Rach, just like your father's was. You'd be a fool to ever forget it. Rachel squelched that niggling little voice as she observed the men end their discussion with a handshake. The Cadillac pulled away from the curb moments later. Matthew held Darcy's hand as they crossed the street together with Hodgepodge leading the way.

Man and dog entered the store. Darcy merely poked her head in to ask if she could stay outside and play with her ball.

"As long as you stay right here, on the sidewalk," Bonnie told her daughter.

Matthew walked over to the counter. "How's it coming?"

Rachel bundled money into a leather bag. It would go into the office safe until it could be taken to the bank. "We're almost done." She didn't want to ask. She didn't. Still, she found herself asking anyway. "Who was that man you were talking with just now?"

One corner of his mouth hitched up. "It was Austin Hendrix, of all people."

"Austin Hendrix," she repeated thoughtfully, frowning. "That name seems familiar, but I can't place it."

"Does Hendrix Hotels ring a bell?"

All at once everything fell into place. "He has several hotels in Southern California, in smaller cities rather than large metropolitan areas, geared for the tourist market."

"Uh-huh. And he's been very successful. I've met him before, at a conference somewhere. He just informed me that his corporation owns the building across the street. It's going to be their newest hotel. Or maybe the oldest," he corrected dryly, ''considering its age. They plan to open it in November.''

Rachel hadn't realized how tense she'd been until she took a deep breath and felt herself relax. Bonnie had obviously been mistaken. There couldn't be anything ominous about a conversation between Matthew and Austin Hendrix.

Could there?

9

THEY HAD FINALLY finished and were ready to close for the day when Bonnie said, "I don't see Darcy. She was out on the sidewalk only a minute ago."

Something in the tone of her voice, even beyond the disturbing words, made Matthew turn from the display of greeting cards he'd straightened. He saw Bonnie's eyes widen with fright, as if she were viewing a ghastly nightmare come true, instead of the peaceful scene visible through the window. A heartbeat later she bolted around the counter and ran toward the entrance.

Instantly caught up in her urgency, he beat her by several steps and yanked the door open just as a child's high-pitched cry pierced the quiet. He was out like a shot, but Hodgepodge brushed against him and zipped past like a launched missile. By the time Matthew rounded the building, heading toward the sound of another cry, the dog was almost at the back of the house.

There was a short wooden fence near the rear of the pink building. It had been erected a few feet before the uneven, gradually sloping ground ended in a sheer cliff. Matthew's heartbeat skyrocketed when he saw Darcy on the far side of the fence, small arms flailing helplessly as she teetered backward toward a deadly two-thousand-foot drop.

He raced ahead, hearing the women's footsteps and terrified exclamations somewhere behind him. Yet, despite his speed, he would have been too late if Hodgepodge hadn't lunged through a gap in the fence, braced four sturdy legs right at the side of the drop and snagged strong teeth into the billowing skirt of Darcy's dress.

Although the thin cotton material immediately started to tear with a harsh, shredding noise, it slowed her descent long enough for Matthew to scale the fence with one continuous forward motion and grab for her, reaching his large hands out to grasp her tiny waist as the skirt ripped down through the hem.

Suddenly he was on his knees, an inch away from the edge, with a sobbing Darcy held tightly in his arms. And he watched, powerless and horrified, as Hodgepodge, abruptly deprived of an opposing force to brace against, scrambled for balance.

And failed.

In an instant that seemed to last a lifetime, the dog plunged over the side of the mountain.

Both women screamed. Matthew ruthlessly suppressed a futile, agonized shout. He couldn't lose control now. With a soothing hand, he gently patted Darcy's back and willed himself to get carefully to his feet. He shielded her against his chest as he turned and walked to the fence.

Bonnie, looking at least ten years older than she had a few moments ago, held her arms out for her daughter. "I'll never be able to thank you enough, Matthew," she said brokenly, clearly fighting for composure so as not to alarm Darcy any further. He reached out one hand to cup her shoulder in a brief, bracing gesture. Then he lifted Darcy over the fence and gave her to Bonnie.

"I just wanted to get my ball, Mommy," the little girl said forlornly as Bonnie turned and carried her away with quick strides. "It rolled down the hill and I couldn't find it and I slipped on a rock and then I slipped again and...and I didn't mean to be bad."

"It's okay, sweetheart. It's okay." Bonnie's reassuring

words grew fainter as she rounded the corner of the building and they were gone.

Silently Rachel climbed the fence and dropped down on the other side. She went straight into Matthew's arms. "I'm so sorry, I'm so sorry," she whispered over and over, as though he needed comfort as badly as she.

Now that the child was out of earshot, he wanted to vent his frustration, to issue every formidable curse he could come up with at his inability to save the dog, but speech proved impossible. The huge, solid, totally unexpected lump that had lodged in his throat wouldn't allow it. So he just held Rachel as closely, as soothingly, as he'd held Darcy.

Just then, while Matthew swallowed hard in an effort to clear his throat, a faint yelp sounded from below. Stunned, he pulled back and met Rachel's astonished, tearful gaze.

"Oh, my God," she said softly. "It can't be."

Another yelp split the silence. "It is," he forced out in a croak. "I don't know how, but it sure the hell is." With that, he grasped her hand in a viselike grip. Together they took quick but careful steps forward and peered over the edge.

Miraculously Hodgepodge was there, several yards beneath them, not only alive but seemingly uninjured.

Against all odds, the dog had landed squarely on top of a large, sparsely leafed bush that grew tenaciously from the side of the mountain. His torso was stretched out crosswise on the persistent plant while his legs dangled over the sides. He moved them again and again in a frenzied attempt to raise himself—a fruitless effort, since all that lay under his paws was a swirling current of summer air and a lethal drop to the valley floor.

The warm jolt of elation pulsing through Matthew abruptly died, wiped out by icy dread when he saw how the dog's feverish activity was swiftly snapping off branches. If that rapid destruction continued, the plant might soon be too weak to bear its burden. Disaster would unquestionably follow.

"Hodgepodge, be still," he commanded firmly. It was a mistake. He realized it the second the dog lifted his head, panted fervently and redoubled his efforts to reach the man he idolized. At this moment, words would be useless to still the animal; instinct had taken over. Only a reassuring touch might be effective enough to save him.

Matthew knew what had to be done. And it had to be done *now*. He inspected the rocky area between the almost level ground where he stood and the bush. It wasn't a totally vertical drop, but it was damn close to it. Still, if he could manage to find some strategic footholds, he'd be able to reach the dog. He had to try.

He turned to Rachel. Judging by her troubled expression as she looked down, she was well aware of the gravity of the situation. "I'm going to try to get to him and calm him before he wrecks his only chance to survive. Go call for help."

Rachel snapped her head up and around to gaze at Matthew. She didn't want to believe what she'd just heard, but the stark determination in his eyes told her he was completely serious. "Matthew, you can't! It's too steep. You might—"

"I have to," he said in a low voice shot through with steel. Before she could say anything further, he caught her to him for a hard kiss, then picked her up in one smooth movement and set her on the other side of the fence. "Go. The sooner you call, the quicker they'll be here."

She wanted to stop him...somehow...some way. To argue. To rage. To seize the front of his white shirt in her fists and hang on to him, if that's what it would take to keep him from risking his life. But he was already seating himself at the edge, positioning his long legs over the side, preparing to descend. The only sensible thing to do was get help.

Fast!

Her heart tripping, Rachel sprinted to the store. She pushed the door open and shouted the situation to an amazed Bonnie, who sat at a table inside the gazebo, holding Darcy on her lap. "Call for help," Rachel ordered in a rush. "I have to get back." Before the last word left her throat, she spun around and returned to the sidewalk. She aimed a quick gaze up and down the street that had been teeming with people an hour earlier. Now the shops were closed, tourists had left. There was no one in sight, and she didn't have time to rap on doors, searching for assistance. If Matthew needed her, she had to be there.

She raced back, praying help would come in time. As she climbed over the fence, her blood froze in her veins when she heard the gravelly clatter of rocks falling, followed immediately by an ominous scrambling noise, a sharp bark and a soft thud. As she dashed to the spot where she'd last seen Matthew, a blue-tinged curse surged up from below. It was the sweetest sound she'd ever heard, because Matthew had been strong enough, alive enough, to make it.

With a rapid glance over the side, Rachel saw that Hodgepodge was no longer alone. Matthew now straddled the lower part of the bush, near the roots. Wedged between a squirming canine body an inch from his chest and the stony mountain wall behind him, he began to pat the dog. "Stay still, pal," he said gently. Instantly the animal quieted.

Rachel felt giddy with gladness at that sight, but it lasted only a moment—only until she noticed that, with the combined weight of man and dog, the bush was gradually tilting downward as more branches broke off and dropped away. She dreaded the need to say what she was about to say, and said it anyway. "Bonnie's getting help, Matthew, but that plant can't hold both of you much longer. They may not get here in time. You might have to…"

He bent his head back until his dark hair met the rocky wall behind him and gazed at her upside down. Even with the distance between them, she saw the grim obstinacy etched on his face. He'd obviously understood the gist of her unfinished statement, for he responded, "No, I'm not letting him go."

Desperately, with tears clouding her vision and her hands balled fiercely enough to bury her nails in her palms, she groped for words to convince him to save himself, if it came to a choice. Whatever else happened, she couldn't lose him.

Oh, God, she couldn't lose him.

Then she heard it: a low rumble invading her frantic thoughts. Soon it grew louder and became the distinct, raucous sound of a motorcycle engine. "I hear someone driving this way," she said. "I'm going to try to stop them. They might be able to help." If Matthew replied to that, she didn't hear it. She was too busy scrambling over the fence, then bolting toward the sidewalk. She had to get there in time. *Had to.*

She did. Speeding toward her when she shot out from between buildings and reached the curb was a rider wearing black from top to toe. At that moment, the big man with the battered cowboy hat looked like an absolute angel to Rachel, and his Harley-Davidson was a glorious chariot. It was Little Earl Dobbs.

Rachel knew that he and Matthew had had a few discussions since they'd fought and formed the beginnings of a friendship right before her eyes. Little Earl might look just as scruffy as he had before, but he'd begun to invest his money wisely.

He pulled over when she waved her arms over her head.

She launched straight into an explanation before he came to a complete stop. Seconds later she was on the back of the cycle and they were headed toward the fence. She climbed it for what seemed like the hundredth time while Little Earl positioned his bike so that it faced away from the edge and pulled a length of rope from a leather saddlebag.

Rachel sank to her knees and looked over the side.

They were still there, exactly as she'd left them; the bush, bless its tenacity, had held.

She hadn't lost him.

Tears of relief flowed down her face as she said, "It was Little Earl. He's going to pull you up with his motorcycle."

The man in black tied a large loop in one end of the rope and dropped it down. "Well, you sure do need a friend today, Matthew," he said with a shake of his head.

Matthew gave him a wry grin. "Little Earl, you look so beautiful right now, I just might kiss you after you get us back up there."

As it turned out, he didn't follow through with that plan. But Rachel did. Once they were all safely on the other side of the fence, and the emergency team that had arrived for the conclusion of the rescue had left, Rachel planted a big kiss smack in the center of Little Earl's lips.

"You don't have to do that with so much enthusiasm," Matthew griped good-naturedly.

She had already kissed Matthew several times with a lot more enthusiasm. She'd also kissed Hodgepodge. And Bonnie and Darcy, who had joined them after the turmoil was over. Now Rachel hugged Little Earl and pulled away. "You have to give me your mother's address," she ordered. "I'm going to wrap up a present and send it to her with my heartfelt thanks for raising a very special son."

"I'll send her a present, too," Darcy offered earnestly, bending her head way back to gaze into the burly man's face. "Do you think she'd like my Slinky? It's really smart. It walks down the steps all by itself."

One corner of Little Earl's mouth hitched up. "I think she'd rather have a picture, if you'd draw one for her."

"Okay. What should I draw?" The two of them and Bonnie immediately became involved in choosing a subject.

Rachel turned to look at Matthew, who had crouched down next to the dog. "You did a great job today, pal," he said softly. "You're going to get a long walk tonight and a huge handful of bones." Hodgepodge barked gleefully and nudged closer to lick Matthew's hard cheek. And, wonder of wonders, he allowed it.

Was he aware that he had stopped calling the dog "mutt" and replaced it with "pal," or had it been done unconsciously? Rachel mused with an inward smile.

Watching them in the slanting crimson rays of the setting sun, she knew she would always remember that moment. The way Matthew's soiled and torn clothes, hopelessly beyond repair, only heightened his attractiveness. The way his hair, streaked with dirt and sweat, hung over his forehead and made him even more appealing. And the way he brushed the dog's droopy ears back and scratched in a special spot with a long-fingered hand that was probably as grimy as it had ever been. All of it—the disarray, the dirt, the sweat—made him downright irresistible, because she'd witnessed the stubborn, heroic effort that had produced it.

Yes, she would remember that moment. Forever.

It was the moment she realized she was in love with Matthew Kent.

RACHEL LONGED TO—had to—convey her feelings somehow and knew that words would be denied her. She couldn't speak of love to a man who didn't even believe in the concept. But she could express her sentiments in another fashion, she decided as she dressed to go out to dinner that evening. She could do it in a way he would welcome: with a physical demonstration. Although he might not perceive the depth of emotion that lay behind her actions, she would know it was there.

As always these days, she wanted to make love with him, but more importantly, tonight she wanted to make love *to* him. Matthew had skillfully taken them both to ecstasy many times over the past week. Now she needed to blaze the trail and take *him*...if she could.

Why was a twenty-nine-year-old woman, married and widowed, still groping her way down life's sensual pathway? she wondered. *Because you married your best friend,* something inside her answered. And all at once she knew it was true.

She had loved Danny McCarthy, would always love him, yet they'd been friends, first and foremost. After several tries, a bit of fumbling and some gentle laughter, they had found sweet fulfillment in their honeymoon bed. Yes, it had been sweet, on that occasion and for the remainder of their life together, but it had not been passion as she now knew it. Undoubtedly Danny hadn't realized it, either. How could he have known? She'd been his only lover, as he'd been hers...until Matthew.

With a last look in the mirror, Rachel made a silent vow. Somehow love had found her again when she'd least expected it; she had to try to seize that chance for happiness. Loving Matthew Kent would be a challenge, she realized.

But tonight she was ready to take on challenges.

THE EVENING STARTED as a celebration. Of life. Of being alive. After a cozy dinner at the House of Joy, an excellent Jerome restaurant occupying a building that had long ago been a bordello, they took Hodgepodge for the promised walk and returned to the store.

At Rachel's suggestion, seconded by a clearly surprised yet completely willing Matthew, they selected something for each other to wear from the intimate apparel section.

With a wicked gleam in his eye, he chose a lacy, dark green chemise so short that what scant covering it afforded would end at the very top of her thighs. "It's going to be a pleasure seeing this on you," he said in a husky voice, his hand lingering over the wispy material as though he were stroking her body.

Determined not to be outdone despite the fact that this kind of sexual banter was totally new to her, she attempted just as wicked a look as she picked up a pair of black silk boxer shorts. "It'll be an equal pleasure—" she snapped the elastic band with a provocatively arched eyebrow "—taking these off you."

He strode forward, until he was so close she could feel his warmth through his dark blue suit. Although his hair was longer now—he hadn't had it cut since he'd arrived in Jerome—his attire reminded her of the day they'd met, when he'd looked like the consummate businessman. Tonight, however, his expression was anything but business-like. "If you keep on talking like that, I can guarantee you we won't even get into these outfits."

She laughed softly and backed away, smoothing a hand down the skirt of the black cocktail dress Bonnie had judged to be "tired." Rachel had planned to wear her new silver-satin slip dress—until Matthew had firmly vetoed that plan. He wanted to enjoy the evening, he'd told her, and not spend it snarling at every man who ogled her. She'd indulged him, because she wanted to indulge him that night. Besides, she thought smugly, he hadn't once looked at her as if he thought anything about her was "tired."

Turning, she walked over to the lotion and potion cabinet. "Surely you can wait a few minutes," she teased as she plucked a small bottle of lotion from a row of massage products. "Especially after that episode in the bathroom." Following everyone's departure just before dusk, they'd gone up to her apartment and engaged in a wildly urgent bout of lovemaking that had started in the shower and ended on the bathroom floor.

"I'm ready again—now," he informed her with a suggestive glance down at the front of his pants, "but I guess I can wait. For a *few* minutes."

She made him wait longer than that.

A lot longer.

SHE WAS DRIVING him right up the wall, Matthew decided nearly an hour later as he lay on his stomach in Rachel's bed and endured the touch of her soft hands moving over his body.

The torture session had begun when she'd appeared from the bathroom in that lacy creation, looking like an unbridled masculine fantasy come true. He'd thought himself so clever in choosing that garment, knowing it would reveal rather than conceal—and envisioning everything that would be revealed.

But he'd suffered mightily almost from the moment he'd seen her in it. Because, dammit, she wouldn't let him remove it and make love to her. "Not yet," she'd told him more than once.

"You're killing me—do you know that?" he ground out, one side of his face flattened against the pillow.

Her chuckle was low, a little lascivious and not at all concerned as she straddled him, her knees pressed to the bed on either side of his hips. The quiver of response that seductive sound generated followed her fingers down his spine. "You're supposed to be enjoying this massage," she purred. "Relax."

He sighed gustily, attempting to follow that directive, and soon concluded it was useless. Relaxation was impossible. Maybe it was the feel of the silk boxer shorts, he mused. He'd always been a strictly cotton man when it came to underwear, but he had to admit there was something undeniably arousing in the way the thin fabric fondled him in places his lover had thus far ignored. Primarily one spot where he dearly desired her attention.

"I have another 'condition,'" he said cajolingly in an effort to hurry things along. It was a wry reference to the morning he'd had breakfast in bed and Rachel for dessert. "Don't you want to help me in my time of need?"

"Not yet," she replied—again!—with amusement so blatant he could virtually see her smile. Shifting position, she kneaded his muscles with a touch that both soothed and roused as she moved lotion-slick hands down his right leg to his ankle, and then up his left leg, just as soothingly and rousingly and tortuously, until she reached the juncture at the top of his thighs.

Fast approaching his limit, he was about to take matters—and Rachel—into his own hands when she slid her fingers under the waistband of his shorts. "Lift up and I'll do the rest of you," she commanded with tender tyranny. Quickly, thankfully, he lifted his hips, and she pulled the silky underwear down his legs and off his feet. He was far past ready to be "done."

Then her hands were on his buttocks, rubbing with a circular motion that caused his heart to skip a beat before it rallied. Almost immediately she began to feather tiny kisses over his shoulders, his back, his waist…and lower, and he held still as long as he could before turning over so craftily she remained astride his thighs when he faced her a swift second later.

"Yes, you do have a condition," she agreed with exaggerated gravity, glancing down at his arousal, her hair flowing over her shoulders the way he liked to see it. Her lips curved in a half smile as she returned her sparkling gaze to his. "But it's not fatal. In fact, I'm positive I can make you all better."

With that welcome diagnosis, she lowered her head and took him into her mouth for the first time. He groaned deep in his throat.

"God, that feels good, witchy woman. Make that great...ah...terrific." Again, this time clenching his jaw in the effort, he held out as long as he could.

It wasn't long.

Intent on her task, enjoying the velvet hardness, the musky taste of him, Rachel felt Matthew's fingers fisting in her hair before a gentle tug pulled her head away from him. She looked up and found his smoky gray eyes regarding her with a stark intensity that told her she could delay no longer.

Not that she really wanted to. She'd been determined to arouse him to a fever pitch; that had clearly been accomplished. She'd seduced the man she loved, and in the process had been seduced herself, she realized. Her breasts were tight, nipples peaked against the airy lace covering them. Wetness had formed between her thighs. She was ready; he was champing at the bit.

Still, she couldn't resist the urge to push his patience a little farther. "Not yet," she murmured with a taunt-the-tiger grin, just to see what he would do.

She found out. Instantly.

In the blink of an eye, she wound up on her back, legs spread widely as he knelt between them. He grabbed the hem of her garment and unceremoniously pulled it up and over her head. With dispatch, he retrieved a condom from the top of the nightstand and dealt with it.

"Now," he said implacably, transforming word to action by entering her with one rapid thrust.

Empowered by the element of surprise, she managed to reverse their positions; their bodies remained joined.

"Now," she echoed. "Tonight I want to take you, Matthew."

As if he understood her need to lead, he nodded without hesitation. "All right. Take me, Rachel. All the way."

And she did. With a soft sigh and a sinuous movement, she started them on the path to satisfaction. It was richer, more gratifying, than any journey they had made before, because this time her love for him paved the way. One of them realized it; the other could only wonder at the difference.

When they reached their destination sharp, sweet, endless moments later, they cried out as one.

MATTHEW PONDERED that curious difference as he lay listening to Rachel's quiet breathing. She was fast asleep, her head resting on his hair-darkened chest. One of her arms hugged his waist; her legs were tangled with his. He was wide awake, holding her close and attempting to analyze what had happened only minutes ago. Something had changed, he knew, beyond the fact that Rachel had taken charge for the first time. Actually, ever since that afternoon there had been a subtle alteration in the way she treated him, reacted to him.

Maybe it was an aftereffect of the gut-wrenching scene at the mountain's edge. After all, she'd been horrified at the child's danger, then badly upset by the dog's fall, and gravely afraid for his own welfare. That trauma was bound to affect her in some way, perhaps even creating those subtle changes he'd noted.

Something inside him had altered, too. At one point, as he'd scrambled over shifting rocks to save himself from a disastrous drop, the thought had flashed through his mind that if he didn't survive, his biggest regret would be that he'd had so little time with Rachel. He'd known her for only a month, been her lover for a week. That time was much, much too short.

But he had survived and things had undeniably changed.

Before today, he had deliberately refused to speculate on what would happen when the six-week period was up and he could leave Jerome, having secured his aunt's estate. Speculation was for dreamers; he preferred certainty. Plans could be made when he completed his objective, he'd resolved.

Now, although he had two weeks to go to achieve his goal, he was certain of one thing: there was no way in hell he could just up and leave Rachel. He hadn't yet determined how he would accomplish it, but he *would* remain her lover. He'd have to give the matter some serious thought. Not that he had any real fear of failure. He was a resourceful man; that hadn't altered.

Nevertheless, the aftermath of near disaster had produced changes—in him and undoubtedly in Rachel, Matthew concluded, feeling his muscles unwind as his body finally began to relax. That had to be the reason for the intriguing difference in the way she looked at him, touched him, made love to him and with him.

Of course that's the reason, Kent, he assured himself.

What else could it be?

LIFE WAS GOOD, Rachel decided when she woke up for the second time on Sunday morning. The day had begun so splendidly. Matthew had woken her at dawn and made long, slow, marvelous love to her. He was gone now—probably out walking Hodgepodge since the apartment seemed very quiet—but before she'd fallen back to sleep, he had promised to serve her breakfast in bed. In fact, he had virtually ordered her not to get up. He was spoiling her, and she loved it.

She loved him.

That was the reason she felt so good, she reflected, snuggling up to a pillow that still held Matthew's tangy male scent. She was in love, and it felt wonderful. Pollyanna though she might be, she was even beginning to conquer doubts about the future. Somehow everything looked brighter today. In his own verbally undemonstrative way, Matthew cared about her. She'd seen it in his eyes when he'd taken her so tenderly in the rising sun's light. It might not be undying love, but it was clearly more than just physical desire between them. He cared about her. She was sure of it.

And he had changed, little by little, from the man who had reluctantly agreed to come to Jerome. Did he realize it? He seemed to be more relaxed—except when he wanted to make love to her!—and he'd had the opportunity to occupy his time with things unrelated to work, like cooking and fishing. Oh, he would never be as blithely free-spirited as Jack. But perhaps, now that he'd gotten along without it for a while, he would want more in his life than just his business. His decision to downsize Kent Enterprises already hinted at that. The real test would come, of course, when he was free to return to Denver. Could there really be a viable chance for them to have a future together? She could come up with no solid answer one way or the other. Yet today she had hope.

Stretching out, Rachel arched her back like a cat and yawned widely. Life was good.

10

"THINGS ARE GOING WELL, pal," Matthew told Hodgepodge as he stirred the fragrant stew simmering over a low flame. They were in the kitchen of the pine cabin that was part of his aunt's estate; the cabin had many conveniences of a larger home, merely on a reduced scale. Matthew was doing most of the cooking for Rachel and himself these days, and enjoying it far more than he once would have considered possible. "You'll have to admit it was a stroke of genius on my part to suggest that we come up here for a week."

Hodgepodge barked enthusiastically.

"Besides having Rachel to myself when Jack's not around—" Matthew glanced out the short window over the sink "—the setting's terrific." This side of Mingus Mountain had a rough, natural charm he found appealing.

He and Rachel had driven over the mountain three days ago, taking the Buick and the sports car so both would have a vehicle during the times Bonnie couldn't mind the store and Rachel had to return to Jerome. This morning had been one of them, but she'd be back by late afternoon. In her absence, he'd spent the morning fishing with Jack, who was staying at his own small cabin a half mile away.

Matthew's expression turned thoughtful. "Something's bothering Jack, pal. Did you notice the way he kept opening his mouth and then snapping it shut today?"

Hodgepodge issued a soft "Woof."

Taking that as a sign of agreement, Matthew added,

"And I don't think he's disturbed by the obvious fact that Rachel and I have become lovers. He looked too pleased when he came for dinner on our first night here. It's something else. Maybe he'll finally get it out when he comes for dinner tonight."

Matthew walked into the cozy living room, the dog trailing him, and sat on a brown leather sofa backed by a group of narrow windows covered by louvered wood blinds. Bright sunlight peeked through their thin slats. He stretched his long, Levi's-clad legs out in front of him and gazed at the painting on the opposite wall. It was another of Luther LaMont's efforts, this time a snowy winter scene. As he looked at the work of art, Matthew's thoughts turned to the future. He'd vowed to continue to be Rachel's lover, and that morning, while he'd been down at the lake sitting next to the curiously silent Jack, the way to accomplish it had hit him.

It was so damn simple.

He didn't have to return to Denver—not permanently, at any rate. Modern technology being what it was, he could establish an operation anywhere…even in Jerome. He needed a sophisticated computer system, a modem, a fax, an independent telephone system with several lines, and an assistant. That was it. Lou Arlington could run the Denver office; he could stay in Jerome. He would still have to travel, of course, but much of the time he could be where he increasingly needed to be.

With Rachel.

He could not only continue their relationship, he could remain in a city he'd become fond of. He liked the friendliness of the people, the way they looked out for one another, the mountainous setting, the crisp, unpolluted air. Everything. He could have all of that. And Rachel McCarthy as his lover.

Things were definitely going well.

Just then the distinctive sound of a sports car's engine could be heard approaching the cabin. There was no squeal of tires as the vehicle turned off the main road, Matthew was pleased to note. Rachel might drive like a bat out of hell in town, he mused, rising, but at least she was careful on these winding mountain roads.

He was walking toward the door, prepared to greet her with a welcoming kiss, when she entered. One glance at her tightly set features, the coldness in her eyes, stopped him in his tracks. Although dressed in a yellow T-shirt and jeans, she looked like an avenging angel who was quite clearly upset. With him.

"What's the matter?"

"You tell me," she said grimly as she walked toward him, stopping inches away. "I met Austin Hendrix today. He pulled up in his Cadillac as I was leaving and asked me to tell you he had mailed you his offer to buy the building—the 'incongruous pink palace,' he called it—just as the two of you had discussed." She swallowed hard. "Aren't you being a little premature, Matthew, selling the place before it's even yours?"

Letting his breath out in a gusty sigh, Matthew lifted a hand and ran it through his hair. Why did this have to happen now? With all that had transpired since, he'd pushed that talk with Hendrix to the back of his mind.

"I'm not selling it," he explained patiently in an attempt to calm her down. "It was just a casual conversation. When he found out I was about to become the owner, he said he wanted to make me an offer. I said, 'Okay, put it in writing.' It happens all the time in business."

"Business," she repeated brusquely, clearly not calmed a bit by his explanation. "Is that all that house means to you—just another thing to make a buck with?"

He felt his patience dwindling at her sarcasm. "You're blowing this way out of proportion, Rachel. It's a piece of property, for Pete's sake. Property is bought and sold all the time.''

''And what about the store?''

''The store could be moved, if it came to that, and the profits from the sale of the house used to relocate. Main Street would be a better location. You pointed that out yourself.''

''But I didn't mean—''

''And I'm not selling, as I tried to tell you before. I'd only consider selling at some point if it were a prudent business decision. I haven't received Hendrix's offer yet, much less had an opportunity to review it.''

''But how can you even consider selling when there's no real need?'' She didn't wait for a reply, she just forged on. ''That house is more than a piece of property. It's more than the store. It's…a part of history. It's Luther LaMont, painting on the back porch and capturing that beautiful view…'' Her words died as she suddenly became absolutely still.

''What the devil is wrong now?'' Matthew asked irritably, seeing something very close to dread enter her gaze.

''Hendrix wants to tear the house down. I should have realized that from the minute he said he'd made an offer. It's the only thing that makes sense. He doesn't want a 'pink palace' blocking the mountain view. The wealthy Mr. Hendrix probably figures that even though Jerome's buildings have National Historic Landmark status, he can get board approval to raze it.'' She paused for a long moment, spearing him with a look from green eyes that had turned as dark as jade. ''How much precious profit would you need, Matthew, to sell to Hendrix and put the wrecking ball in motion?''

That was the last straw. His restraint toppled like a load of massive beams stacked too high. Because he had to put some distance between them—or shake her—he turned sharply and strode across the room, his boot heels pounding on the pine-plank floor. He pivoted to face her when he was several feet away.

"I've taken all I'm going to take from you, Rachel. I will not stand by and let you imply that I'd be willing to do anything for a dollar. Nobody gets away with that, do me hear me?" His voice was deadly soft. *"Nobody."*

Rachel had once wondered what she would do if his formidable temper were ever directed at her. Now she knew.

She got as mad as blazes herself.

Planting her hands on her hips, she met his thunderous glare head-on with a look that would singe iron. "What the hell am I supposed to think? You clearly don't care a whit about a very special house that's become my home. You'd sell it, even though—"

"I explained that I might—*might*—sell it someday," he interjected, "but only under certain conditions. Only if it were a prudent—"

"You can take prudence and stuff it!" After that near shout, her voice turned as deadly quiet as his. "And you can take our relationship and...stuff it, too. I was beginning to think we might have a future together, optimist that I am, until those rose-colored glasses were knocked off with a vengeance. At this moment, I'm seeing stark reality and I hate the view." She took a deep breath. "Serves me right for being fool enough to fall in love with a man who doesn't believe in love."

Surprise flashed across his face. Ignoring the rest of her words, he slowly moved closer and said, "You love me."

"Yes," she admitted soberly, "but you can't afford my love." She crossed her arms beneath her breasts, hiding hands that had begun to tremble. "To put it in business terms, Matthew, love is expensive. The price is serious emotional commitment, and love in return. You have neither commodity.''

"I was honest with you about that," he reminded her.

"And I told you I'd take what you could offer. I remember. Now I find I want—need—more. I need it all."

"So, you're ending it," he said curtly. "Just like that."

She remained silent because her throat was suddenly too tight to talk; she was very close to tears yet determined not to let them fall. She wouldn't break down in front of him.

Matthew's hard mouth twisted. "I care about you, Rachel. But apparently that's not enough. Well, you can rest easy about me getting my mercenary hands on the house. It'll never be mine. I'm out of here." Whipping around, he started for the bedroom.

Hodgepodge, who had watched their confrontation while sprawled out on a small braided rug in front of the sofa, jumped up to follow.

Rachel knew what Matthew had to mean, yet she couldn't quite believe it. "You're going back to *Denver?*"

"You're damn right I am!" he growled as he walked through the bedroom door. A second later he slapped his suitcase on the bed with enough force to be heard in the living room. It was swiftly succeeded by the sound of drawers being wrenched open and slammed shut.

He's leaving, she thought numbly, sitting down on the sofa. With a little over a week to go to gain his inheritance, he was leaving, and he'd looked like neither hell nor high water could stop him. *She* couldn't, she was certain. But then, what would be the point, anyway? He didn't need Ava's estate. He had plenty of money, a business and a life waiting for him in Denver.

Matthew stalked back into the room. "I'll stop at the store to pack up the rest of my things," he told her as he crossed to the outside door, not even glancing her way. When he opened it, Hodgepodge, who'd been one step behind him, moved forward. Matthew leaned over and put a hand on the dog's collar, halting him. He set his suitcase aside, then crouched down. "No, you can't come with me, pal. You have to stay here and become the richest dog in town."

As if he knew exactly what was being said, Hodgepodge whimpered mournfully and licked Matthew's hand.

"I'm sorry, pal," he said softly. "I'd take you with me if I could. But I can't." He got up. "Stay," he ordered.

Hodgepodge whimpered again, but obeyed.

Just before closing the door, Matthew turned and met Rachel's solemn gaze for an instant. Then he was gone.

Hodgepodge approached Rachel, bleak sorrow in his black eyes, looking as bereft as she felt. She knelt on the rug and wrapped her arms around him in an effort to comfort him, but he was the one who comforted her when she put her arms around him. She buried her face in his furry neck, needing to hold on to something, because her world had just fallen apart.

That was the way Jack found her twenty minutes later.

MATTHEW SPED DOWN a two-lane, twisting highway cut through a sheer wall of crimson rock. He had stopped in Jerome only long enough to retrieve the rest of his belongings. Now he was twenty miles north of that city, headed toward Flagstaff. The area he drove through was spectacularly beautiful—and spectacularly wasted, in this case, because he noticed little of it.

In just over an hour, he'd be beyond the hundred-mile limit imposed by the will and it would all be over. Except it wouldn't be over, he thought, crushing his foot down on the accelerator to send the Buick surging forward. He would have the memories of the woman he'd left behind to haunt him. *Rachel in his lap the first time he'd kissed her. Rachel's face, drawn with worry, looking down at him from the edge of the mountain. Rachel telling him she loved him, but he couldn't afford her love.* Those images had haunted him for twenty miles…and he couldn't outrun them.

Then why are you running away, Kent? That question came from somewhere inside. It jarred him, but his temper had cooled enough, aided by a stiff breeze blowing in through the open car window, to allow him to consider the matter logically. Running away? Was that what he was doing?

Long, pensive moments later, he came to an inescapable conclusion: running away was exactly what he was doing. Even worse, he was breaking the resolution he'd made to spend six weeks in Jerome. He was quitting, and he had never been a quitter. Was he going to become one now?

Matthew eased up on the accelerator and let out a deep, jagged breath. He had to go back. That was another inescapable conclusion. Despite what had happened today between Rachel and himself, he had to go back and complete the six weeks. It wasn't the estate at stake. It was his self-respect.

He had to return to Jerome.

That decision made, he was searching for a spot wide enough to make a U turn on the narrow road when he saw a vehicle racing down a steep hill off to the right. It was an ancient Jeep, several yards in front of him and kicking up a huge cloud of red dust on its almost vertical path to the road.

"Who in the…" he murmured. Then he had the answer as he recognized the driver. It was Jack. And they were on a collision course.

Matthew stomped on the brakes and narrowly missed rear-ending the other vehicle as it hit bottom and swerved onto the road. With a vicious curse, he wrenched the Buick's steering wheel to the right and pulled off the highway, thudding over small rocks to come to a stop. Executing the same maneuver, Jack stopped several feet down the road.

Matthew shot out of the car and stalked to the Jeep. He was angry all over again. "What the hell do you think you're doing?" he roared at his uncle.

Jack got out. "Trying to stop you from making the biggest mistake of your life, you idiot," he roared in return. A slam of the Jeep's door punctuated that statement.

"What the devil difference does it make to you?"

"I may be crazy, but I care about you," Jack muttered.

As they glowered at each other for a tense moment through traces of swirling dust, Matthew saw the underlying concern etched on his uncle's bearded face and knew it was true. Jack cared. That knowledge thwarted his anger. "You could be killed pulling a stunt like that," he said in a milder tone.

"You could get socked on the jaw for leaving Rachel in the shape I found her. I'd do it, too, if you weren't looking as ghastly now as she did then." With that terse reply, Jack walked over to a small boulder and perched on top of it. "Come on, sit down," he said more calmly, waving a hand toward a nearby boulder. "I want to talk to you."

So he's finally going to get it out, Matthew thought, sitting where Jack had suggested. He set his booted feet on the rocky ground and fixed his attention on the other man.

"I never had any intention of telling you...what I'm about to tell you," Jack began, "but over the past couple of weeks and after a lot of thought, I've come to the conclusion that this is something you *have* to know. There's no easy way to say it, so I'll just spit it out." He hesitated for a mere instant. "Matt, your father wasn't the man you believe him to be—an honorable man. At one time in his life, he was a far-from-ethical businessman—" Jack reached in a shirt pocket and pulled out a long manila envelope, folded in half and creased with age "—and I have the documents to prove it."

Although Matthew remained silent, the impact of that startling statement ripped through him, twisting his gut. He wanted to shout that it couldn't be true...yet he knew it was. There was no denying the stark certainty that had underlined his uncle's words, and apparently there was written proof to back it up. Every muscle in his body tensed as Jack continued.

"Andrew Kent and I disagreed on most everything—except the value of a man's personal integrity. He was very big on integrity. In fact, he touted it so loudly that after a while I began to get suspicious. That's why, when the cook your parents employed decided to leave, I suggested a replacement to my sister and asked her not to tell Andrew who had made the recommendation. Rosalind assumed it was because her husband would immediately reject any person I recommended—and he undoubtedly would have—but my motives went beyond getting an acquaintance a job. I wanted to insert someone I could trust in the household. And my friend Erica Hanson was hired. Do you remember her, Matt?"

Matthew nodded thoughtfully, but didn't say anything.

"I asked Erica to be on the outlook for anything unusual," Jack went on, "and she picked up on a curious phone conversation relating to a particular stock transaction, probably because Andrew didn't think a mere servant within hearing distance was anyone to worry about. After Rosalind died, he grew even more careless, and Erica was able to learn more. Using the information she gave me as a beginning, I investigated further. None of what I discovered was strictly against the law—Andrew was too shrewd for that—but there were undeniably questionable trading practices that would certainly have created a great deal of embarrassment for him and damaged his stature in the business community.

"If your mother had still been alive, I would have given the information to her. I don't think it would have come as much of a surprise. She wasn't terribly happy with your father, and it would have given her the means to get him to agree to an uncontested divorce, if she decided to leave him, and allow her to get custody of you without a battle." Jack paused. "But Rosalind was gone, so I wrote out the details, put them in this envelope with supporting documents, and told no one."

"Why?" Matthew had to ask.

"Because I wanted a way to protect you."

Stunned, Matthew couldn't believe he had heard correctly. *"To protect me?"*

"That's right. Your mother was gone. You were alone with Andrew, and I didn't quite trust him to be a good father to you. Since he already had a good start on accumulating wealth and the power it breeds, I wanted to have some hold over him if he ever mistreated you. I was no longer welcome in the house, but Erica gave me regular reports on you. After a few years, however, it became obvious that Andrew would never harm you physically. You were too valuable to him. You were the heir to the Kent empire. So I stopped worrying about you." Jack's expression turned grim. "But I shouldn't have, because you were hurt in ways I only began to understand as we got to know each other."

"What are you—" Matthew started to say.

Jack broke in. "I'm talking about the way Andrew raised you in his image. You can follow in his rational-at-all-costs, unemotional footsteps, Matt, but I believe you're capable of much more. There's a good woman who clearly loves you back at that cabin. If you let her get away, you're a damn fool."

Jack got up and walked over to hand the envelope to Matthew. "I thought many times about putting a match to this, but something always held me back. Now the choice is yours. You can read it, or you can burn it unread and forget it ever existed. I'll never mention it again, or tell another soul. But it's the truth, and I can't say I'm sorry I told you. No life should be built on a lie."

Still coming to grips with what he'd just learned, Matthew rose to his feet. He already knew what he had to do. "I'll read it...and then I'll burn it." He put the envelope in his pocket.

Jack studied him intently. "Do you hate me for telling you?"

Matthew shook his head. "One thing I've always valued is honesty. I know it wasn't easy to tell me, Jack, but you're right—no life should be built on a lie...and I'm afraid too much of mine has."

"Where will you go now?"

Running one hand through his windblown hair, Matthew said, "I'm going back to Jerome. Actually I was about to turn around when you showed up. I'd already figured out that I couldn't just quit. But after what you've told me, I have a lot of things to consider."

"And Rachel?"

And Rachel? Their relationship was the most vital thing he had to consider. "Tell her I'll be there waiting for her...whenever she's ready to come home."

RACHEL PULLED UP in front of the store. From his seat by her side, Hodgepodge poked his head out the partially open car window and panted fervently. Obviously her companion was glad to be back. She was less sure of her feelings.

They had spent the past two days alone at the cabin, after Jack had reappeared on Friday night with some astonishing news: Matthew had not gone to Denver; he had returned to

Jerome. He'd be waiting for her, Jack had said, when she was ready to come home. Well, she wasn't at all sure she was ready, but she was here.

Why had Matthew come back? That question had plagued her unceasingly. Was it only to finish the six weeks? Or was there more to his decision?

Stop speculating and go find out, she told herself, squaring her shoulders before opening the driver's door. She wasn't a coward, even though she'd needed two days to get herself back together enough to face him with composure.

Hodgepodge followed her out to the street. A second later he was at the store entrance, waiting for her to open the door. She used her key to enter, since it was Monday and the store was closed. The bell chime greeted her merrily. Instantly the dog left her, racing through the store and down the back hall. A second later he began to bark joyously.

Rachel was aware of that cheerfully raucous sound on one level; on another, her mind was captured by the sight that met her wide-eyed gaze. She couldn't believe it!

There were silver-framed eyeglasses. With rose-colored lenses. Everywhere.

Hundreds of them.

They decorated all areas of the store—propped up on shelves, racks, tables, cabinets, counters...even the gazebo.

Matthew had done this. She knew that by the way they'd been precisely positioned—just so far apart and not a millimeter farther—by a sternly meticulous hand.

"Welcome back, Rachel," a low voice said.

She saw him then, standing in the doorway to the back hall, dressed in his "casual" outfit of white shirt and gray pants. Hodgepodge was at his side.

She'd agonized for hours over what she would say to

him. Now, the words came easily. "You love me," she told him with quiet assurance.

His brows shot up as he moved toward her. "How did you know that when I've just begun to figure it out myself?"

She walked straight into his arms. "I knew it the moment I saw all those eyeglasses lined up in those tidy rows." She laid her head against his broad shoulder; his long fingers brushed gently through her hair. "How were you able to get so many exactly alike?"

"I called the largest distributor in Phoenix and flat-out demanded that they sell me their entire stock." He pulled back slightly and looked down at her with something in his eyes she had never seen before.

"It's my way of saying that I want Rosie the Optimist back. I want her to put on those invisible rose-colored glasses and help me view a little of the world through them. I want her to teach me about love, and I promise to be a fast learner." He paused for a heartbeat. "I have a lot of things to tell you—things about the past Jack told me a few days ago that made me take a hard look at my life. But right now, the future is more important. I want you to marry me, Rachel. I want to live in this pink house with my store-keeper wife and a bunch of rowdy kids. I want—need—it all."

Rachel smiled softly, knowing her love for him showed plainly in her gaze. "How can I possibly refuse a man romantic enough to do something like...this?" she mused, indicating the eyeglasses all around them with a wave of her hand.

His dark brows went up again. "*I'm* romantic?"

"You better believe it. Just like the hero in a romance novel."

"I'll be damned."

"So I guess I'll have to accept your proposal, Mr. Kent."

Swiftly Matthew covered her mouth with his, and they sealed that bargain with a long, deep kiss that went on and on. "Now all we have to decide is what to do with the eyeglasses," he said when he finally raised his head.

"We'll come up with something."

"Indeed we will, witchy woman. Later." He scooped her up in his arms. "After I make love to you. I think we should try the gazebo."

"The *gazebo!*"

A frankly wicked grin appeared on his face. "I can't wait to see you wearing nothing but a pair of rose-colored glasses."

She made him wear a pair, too.

Epilogue

THE WEDDING was held on a Monday afternoon at the Realm of Romance. Each guest received a pair of rose-colored glasses, compliments of the bride and groom. A good portion of the citizens of Jerome attended, overflowing the store and spilling out onto the sidewalk. Luckily it was a perfect October day—crisp and cool, yet not too cold.

Little Earl bought a new black cowboy hat for the occasion. Louise Arlington flew in from Denver to cheerfully offer her best wishes.

Dirk Dahlstrom had been invited, but couldn't attend due to other commitments. He did, however, send a stunningly huge basket of pink roses with a small card that read:

> Congratulations. I wish you much happiness,
> lovely Rachel. Glad you finally wised up, Kent.
>
> Dirk

The ceremony itself took place inside the gazebo, with Bonnie as matron of honor and Jack as best man.

William Wilson gave his daughter away for the second time. He had arrived two hours before the start of the festivities. "I was determined to get it right this time, honey," he'd told Rachel, referring to his tardiness at her first wedding.

She'd gone into his arms and hugged him, hard and long, heedless of wrinkling her green silk-brocade dress. "I'm determined to do better, too, Dad," she'd said, vowing to pursue the closeness so long absent. It was a day for new beginnings.

Father and daughter smiled at each other, starting to forge that new relationship as they walked down the aisle cleared between the store's displays. Matthew, looking so handsome in his tuxedo that Rachel's heart turned over at the sight, waited for them.

Later Rachel and Matthew danced their first dance together as husband and wife to "I Can't Help Falling In Love With You" played over the speaker system. When the song ended, Benjamin Bradford, another of their guests, approached them.

"Could I speak to you both alone for a minute?" the dignified man asked. He was smiling, yet something in his demeanor hinted of more serious matters.

The second-floor apartment was the closest private spot. The front half was in the process of being remodelled into a high-tech office for Matthew. The rear bedroom and kitchen would remain, so that Jack would have a place to stay when he was in Jerome. Rachel, Matthew and Hodgepodge occupied the third floor.

"This will only take a moment," Bradford said when they'd entered and closed the door. "I have something for both of you...from Ava." With that startling announcement, he reached into the breast pocket of his navy suit and pulled out an envelope. He handed it to Matthew. "When you read this, you'll understand why I waited until today to give it to you. I'll leave you two alone now, but I'll be glad to answer any questions you might have later. I think you'll find it...interesting." Giving them a slyly pleased look, Bradford departed.

With a what-in-the-world? glance at Rachel, Matthew opened the envelope. He unfolded the single sheet enclosed, then put an arm around her to draw her closer. Together they read the letter penned on lavender paper.

Dear Matt and Rachel,

Since Ben Bradford has given you this note, I will assume that you decided to spend six weeks in Jerome, Matt, and have now married my very dear friend.

Rachel, I always felt you deserved a second chance at love and thought you just might find it with my nephew. So Ben and I hatched a plot to bring you two together. You deserve the best and, since he's half McCarthy, I believe Matt is the best.

Matt, I'm sorry we never had the chance to really know each other. You were a cute kid at four, and I'll bet you're a handsome man now. But then, all the McCarthy men are good-looking. Enjoy your life with Rachel and the children I dearly hope you will have, and raise a toast to your "flighty" Aunt Ava every once in awhile.

Be happy. Life is too short to be anything else.

Ava

P.S. Kiss Hodgepodge for me. He was a wonderful companion, but if you really think I would be crazy enough to leave my estate to a dog, I'll let you in on another secret. I named you both as joint trustees of the trust to be established for Hodgepodge. That way, I had one more chance to get you two together!

Rachel looked up at her husband. "We were set up," she said. The beginnings of a soft smile curved her lips.

Matthew nodded ruefully as he gazed down at his wife. "We sure were—" he caught her in a tight embrace "—and I couldn't be happier. I love you, Rachel. You're absolutely the right woman for me."

"You're the right man for me, Matthew," Rachel murmured, holding him close. "I'm every bit as happy as you are."

And it was true.

Their love had built them a bridge to happiness.

HARLEQUIN WOMEN KNOW ROMANCE WHEN THEY SEE IT.

And they'll see it on **ROMANCE CLASSICS**, the new 24-hour TV channel devoted to romantic movies and original programs like the special **Romantically Speaking—Harlequin™ Goes Prime Time.**

Romantically Speaking—Harlequin™ Goes Prime Time introduces you to many of your favorite romance authors in a program developed exclusively for Harlequin® readers.

Watch for **Romantically Speaking—Harlequin™ Goes Prime Time** beginning in the summer of 1997.

If you're not receiving ROMANCE CLASSICS, call your local cable operator or satellite provider and ask for it today!

ROMANCE CLASSICS

Escape to the network of your dreams.

See Ingrid Bergman and Gregory Peck in *Spellbound* on Romance Classics.

Take 4 bestselling love stories FREE

Plus get a FREE surprise gift!

Special Limited-time Offer

Mail to Harlequin Reader Service®

P.O. Box 609
Fort Erie, Ontario
L2A 5X3

YES! Please send me 4 free Harlequin Love and Laughter™ novels and my free surprise gift. Then send me 4 brand-new novels every other month, which I will receive months before they appear in bookstores. Bill me at the low price of $3.24 each plus 25¢ delivery per book and GST*. That's the complete price and a savings of over 10% off the cover prices—quite a bargain! I understand that accepting the books and gift places me under no obligation ever to buy any books. I can always return a shipment and cancel at any time. Even if I never buy another book from Harlequin, the 4 free books and the surprise gift are mine to keep forever.

302 BPA A7TR

Name _____ (PLEASE PRINT)

Address _____ Apt. No. _____

City _____ Province _____ Postal Code _____

This offer is limited to one order per household and not valid to present Love and Laughter™ subscribers. *Terms and prices are subject to change without notice. Canadian residents will be charged applicable provincial taxes and GST.

CLL-397   ©1996 Harlequin Enterprises Limited

Don't miss these Harlequin favorites by some of our top-selling authors!